BROTHER CARNIVAL

BROTHER CARNIVAL

A NOVEL

DENNIS MUST

...

ILLUSTRATIONS

RUSS SPITKOVSKY

Red Hen Press | *Pasadena, CA*

Book design by Ann Basu

Library of Congress Cataloging-in-Publication Data
ISBN: 978-1-59709-684-3

The National Endowment for the Arts, the Los Angeles County Arts Commis-sion, the Ahmanson Foundation, the Dwight Stuart Youth Fund, the Max Factor Family Foundation, the Pasadena Tournament of Roses Foundation, the Pasadena Arts & Culture Commission and the City of Pasadena Cultural Affairs Division, the City of Los Angeles Department of Cultural Affairs, the Audrey & Sydney Ir-mas Charitable Foundation, the Kinder Morgan Foundation, the Meta & George Rosenberg Foundation, the Allergan Foundation, and the Riordan Foundation partially support Red Hen Press.

   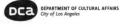

First Edition
Published by Red Hen Press
www.redhen.org

It's as if there is little in life that makes any recognizable sense; and the pathway to inner peace—or to God, if you prefer— is to rejoice in what especially doesn't.

BOOK ONE

PRELUDE

Ethan Mueller   November 13, 1956
142 Westover Street
Pittsburgh, Penn.

Dear Ethan,

Enclosed is Westley's last communication, having arrived, once
again, with neither a salutation nor a return address, several
months later than the story collection I gave you on Sunday.

    If you are reading this letter, I'm deeply relieved . . . and gather
you've decided to pursue the quest. His "Going Dark" might assist
you more than the others.

Love,

Papa

* * *

"Going Dark" was the last of the many works of short fiction that Christopher Daugherty, a pseudonym, published in various literary journals in the early decades following World War II. Since fiction writers often seek inspiration for their work from their own lives, from this story and others, I have endeavored to piece together his true identity.

What follows will reveal why.

GOING DARK
by
Christopher Daugherty

I am an aging actor. Well, I was one, but I seldom get opportunities to audition any longer. When I do, I'm rarely called back.

Actors are notorious prevaricators. There's a simple explanation for this: we like to think of ourselves as a *tabula rasa* until the script or dialogue is in hand. That's when we come to life. But it isn't ours. Luigi Pirandello wrote about such matters.

So if you were to ask, say, *Where do you live?*—I would lie, recall my most recent role, and offer that person's address.

How many children do you have? Then I must think back to when I played a father and answer: six. He was a German soldier in a little-known World War II drama I starred in Off-Off-Broadway. His name was Josef, and he'd hidden his Waffen-SS uniform under the attic floorboards for fear that it would be discovered by one of his offspring.

And your wife—who is she? I've had many, but then I picture the comeliest, Alana, whose raven-black hair she'd braid in one glorious plait. When she climbed the stairs to bed at night, I'd watch it sweep from the left side of her porcelain back to the right, pendulum-like. In a pre-Technicolor film, I'd taken her home to my widowed mother, who lived in Ohio. That evening, when Alana retired to my old bedroom, Mama inquired if she was a "Jewess."

Immediately, I visualized my uniform up in our attic. But there was no attic. And my surname is Daugherty. Well, it was anyway, in a television commercial where I played the bank manager, Christopher Daugherty. When we'd wrapped up the one-day shoot, walking out of the studio famished, I laughed to myself. I hadn't a dime in my pocket. If I had borrowed the bespoke three-piece suit and those to-die-for calfskin cap-toe shoes I wore, posing before a Chippendale desk, I could have passed myself off in a restaurant as someone of means. When the check arrived, I'd feign I'd left my wallet in my Bank of North America office and would return posthaste with cash.

"And your name, sir?"

"Daugherty . . . Christopher Daugherty." I'd grimace to the waiter. "My wife, Alana, who comes in here often, will be mortified to hear what I've done."

Then I'd gather my overcoat and gesture, *Be right back*. But where did I put it? I remember seeing it, a camel's hair model with bone buttons, on a coat tree alongside the desk. And wasn't there a hat also—a felt, narrow-brim Dobbs? Did I forget that?

Christ, Alana will think I'm losing my mind.

Will she inform the neighbor, Mrs. Mueller, who periodically knocks on our side door and hands Alana a tuna fish casserole she's prepared? The two women talk as if they're old friends. But how could they be? Beatrice Mueller is Josef's wife. She must know what he's secreted above their bedroom ceiling. She complains to Alana of severe migraines. Alana commiserates. Of course, I know why she has headaches.

I've suffered from one ever since I watched a chiaroscuro Nazi movie as a twelve-year-old. Except when I took on that cinematic role, I was a graduate student at the University of Southern California, smoking cigarettes and seeing women. Not Alana—I hadn't had the pleasure of meeting her yet. But I knew it would happen one day because, as I ran through them, the women kept growing lovelier. Once the studio technicians applied my makeup, I was genuinely frightened with what I saw in the mirror. A good ten years had been lopped off my life. And with them the anxieties of adolescence returned within minutes. From puberty through my early teens, I'd suffered this inexplicable anguish that I was about to die. In fact, there was this character in my head who owned a basso profundo voice—it could have been Josef Mueller—lecturing me how utterly stupid life was and insisting that to save me hurt and heartache I must "leap off a trestle bridge," of which there were several in our town.

So in truth, I was an adult, looking twelve and having to relive the torment that I would commit suicide if I was honest with myself. Mama—she could have been the one I mentioned who called Alana a Jewess—preached that to be true to myself, I had to follow my conscience to the letter. Except now my conscience turned out to be a German SS officer who, paralyzed by guilt, had secreted his uniform under the attic floorboards, instructing me to off myself. *"Just fucking do it, Tom!"* he'd command.

But my name wasn't Tom. I mean, it isn't today. My name could be any one of these characters who is not prepared to die inside an aging actor . . . *me*.

Already pitched up because of the mirror incident, I was filmed heading off to the movies with my father on a winter evening during the height of World War II, when air-raid blackouts in the neighborhood were quite common.

Papa, whose name was Philip, bought us popcorn, and we sat in the balcony of a rococo movie house, second row. It, too, was a black-and-white film. The script stipulated that I was possessed by fear that the Germans were going to bomb our small mill town just as they were blitz-krieging London at the time. The Waffen-SS officers appeared on the screen, twenty feet taller than Papa, in jodhpurs, gleaming boots, and officers' caps with black patent leather bills and silver skull emblems on their crowns. Several wore gold-rimmed glasses. Headlights from their ebony motor cars reflected off the spectacles' lenses, shooting sparks of phosphorescence across the screen. At that very moment, the real me and the celluloid me coalesced.

I knew exactly what Josef, my conscience, looked like.

I'd been unable to picture him earlier when he cajoled me on my way to school to forgo classes and accompany him off one of the bridges spanning the dark Neshannock River that ran through our hometown. "Tell me what you look like," I'd stall. "I have to see you, to look you in the eyes, if I'm to believe you're for real. Otherwise I won't listen."

* * *

But portraying this young spectator in the movie house, I *saw* my conscience. He wore a Waffen-SS uniform and wire-rimmed glasses with oval lenses that penetrated the soul. When he removed his officer's cap, the moon reflected off his brilliantined hair. One of my finest performances, the director, Ernst Kirchner, exclaimed, adding that he'd never experienced a more authentic melding of actor and character.

I played it as if it were nothing.

* * *

But now that I'm in the last stage of my life and considering the scant roles that I might perform, it's not simply that boyhood memory that haunts me. The numerous other characters I've performed have memories, too.

The marquee ones hang like so many suits in my closet. There are the winter weights and the summer weights. The bit roles reside in my bureau drawers alongside fading bow ties and dress shirts yellowing at the collar. It's how I recall their personas. Costumes, uniforms, changes of shirts or ties or even underwear—the silk kind, or practical cotton briefs. Some roles I even compare to the shoes lining my closet floor. How a certain individual walked, or how big I thought his feet were. If he was inclined to have an effeminate side . . . the white-and-black spectators are stored on a higher shelf for him. The footwear's leather has begun to crack, not unlike the film clips I've stored in tin canisters in the attic.

As I lie about my small room in Riverside Suites, just south of Columbia University and a block east of the West End Bar (I once saw Ginsberg and Thomas Merton pettifogging there), hoping for a call to some casting, or while I scour *Variety*, it's not just me in attendance. They are sitting waiting, too. Some are on the windowsill smoking or alongside me in bed, watching the traffic outside. Others, with their coats and hats on, are at the door in case a call should come so they can be the first out.

And since I am a blank slate—at least I was one in the beginning, *bereshit bara Elohim*—they won't let me be. In fact, they squabble among themselves.

Every role I've ever performed is now rising up because they can see where this is all headed. *I'm going to die soon.* Christ, does that word send them into a dither. They stir nervously about the room, sharing smokes. Their chatter is a raucous din that causes me to lose even more sleep.

* * *

I've begun to anticipate what will unfold.

It involves a couple of the more prominent characters I've played, those where I channeled Stanislavski, say, like Brando and Dean. You would've exclaimed, *Josef, you were magnificent!* If Alana were here, she'd confess to you how I broke her damned and precious heart.

These stars are packed and ready to go. They're the ones who have begun to aggressively assert themselves in the scarce days, months, perhaps a year or two that I have remaining. Of course, we are all doomed. When I go, they go. But these personas are not about to exit gently.

One keeps urging, *Go up into the attic and get my film. Pull out the projector from the closet and watch me again. That's who you are, Josef. I live in that canister. It's number four, dated 1968. God, I was magnificent then, don't you recall?* Then, as if he were sticking his celluloid tongue in my ear, he whispers, *These others are imposters. We can live again. Watch me, Josef. Bring me back alive.*

We can do great things together. We'll go to a thrift shop and dress me up again. Don't you recall how elegant I looked in that white linen two-piece suit in white shoes and the foulard that looked like a Gauguin Tahitian print?

And we'll find Alana. I swear I'll help you. That will bring us alive again.

We can do it all over.

Screw these other characters hanging around as if they are in a union hall, waiting for the phone to ring.

We make our own phones ring, Josef. Believe me.

And there's something else I've been meaning to tell you now that I can see the blood circulating in your face again. You're listening to me, aren't you? Yes, friend. Now listen up. Alana. You know where she is? In Argentina, Josef.

Does it surprise you?

She's living among those expatriates. Do I need to name them for you? Their kind never die.

Why do you look at me so?

* * *

As if I were a casting director, each day another makes his or her pitch.

Oh, I've played the gentler sex in my time, too. Quite convincingly, in fact. I've even wondered if, had I performed more women's roles, I'd be in the fix I'm in now. With a man, they see what they see.

It wasn't always this way.

But it truly is too late.

I finally don't much care if the phone rings or a part comes my way. I rather enjoy being *nobody* . . . and *nobody* desiring my services.

But these characters flitting about, cuddling up to me during the long nights—they want to live in the worst goddamn way.

That's what terrifies me.

The source of my deep anguish.

One morning I'm afraid I'll mount the attic stairs with a crowbar and pry out the floorboards' ten-penny nails, then step into my moth-eaten Waffen-SS uniform, boots, jodhpurs, patent leather visor cap . . . the full emblematic works. Lift down the crop that I've hidden in the rafters and, after brushing off the years of dust, snap it against my beefy thighs and then tramp back down into my room and announce to all the others their fate.

They know what it is. There will be weeping and gnashing of teeth. Then I will head down the apartment stairwell, parade through the marble lobby, and go out onto the street to begin hunting for my lovely, my darling, my porcelain-skinned Alana, whose neck blushes a rose red before her cheeks do.

What is there to be afraid of? I will cry at the top of my lungs.

And bystanders will drop jeweled rings and eyeglasses in his wake.

PART ONE

CHAPTER ONE

THE MEETING

It was a weekend in September when I decided that what I was about to do must occur prior to daybreak the following Monday. I believed that I owed a final goodbye to my father and didn't want to leave a note for fear that it might never be read.

One may expect I would have gone instead to my devout mother. Better that she explain it to herself after the act, I reasoned, rather than confront the dark truth head-on. Having spent my formative years in her shadow, and being their only child, it was no surprise to friends or family how I chose to spend my life.

My resolve drew breath the Sunday morning an elderly widow waited behind in the sanctuary while I stood at its door bidding good day to the congregants.

It was a new pastorate for me in a farming community parish comprising three dozen or so members, none of whom had inquired about my past. Each Sunday one of the women, unseen, placed a cooked meal at my study door. I'd look out across the faces during the service, imagining who it might be. But my impulse was innocent, for I solemnly assumed the role as their shepherd.

Until that week I had awakened to an emerging crisis of faith. Initially, it wasn't that I doubted the existence of God but was tormented by an insidious will to suspect the miraculous Virgin Birth. I consoled myself by repeating, "This too shall pass." But once the doubting commenced, each passing day it felt like the whole foundation of my faith had begun to crumble.

Then, it was as if God himself appeared before me one evening, challenging, *Why not me?*

And I replied, *Why not?*

Come morning, there was only myself, and I knew not who he was.

That Sunday when I ascended the pulpit, I looked out over the expectant parishioners and froze. Panic-stricken, I blurted, "Let us pray." But no homilies came forth. I raised my head, gesturing that I was at a loss for what to do, but the congregation's heads remained bowed. Occasionally someone looked up and, seeing me staring in anguish at them, would bend back down.

Then a church elder raised his head and mouthed—*Say Amen.*

But how could I?

I was an imposter standing there before them . . . and sought refuge by returning to the pastor's chair.

Now several heads were lifted, gesturing—*Say Amen.*

One crusty old farmer volubly uttered, "*For Chrissake, say AMEN!*"

Finally I stood and cried the word.

At that moment, I experienced an epiphany: Parson Ethan Mueller was but a mere ingredient in their hallowed Sabbath ritual.

Oh, I understood that the congregants didn't view me that way any more than how I perceived the esteemed role I played in their lives. But it could have been virtually anybody on that pulpit—*and in truth, wasn't I?*

I concluded the service by reading a sermon lifted from a homiletics text off my shelves that morning. A hot lunch still awaited me in the pews.

Ina Gresham's husband, Jacob, had passed away that spring. Once all the parishioners had departed, I sat down alongside her. It was immediately apparent that she was in distress.

"What is it, Ina? What is troubling you?"

"I've lost my will to live," she said. Unlike Jacob she chose her words sparingly.

I sat there mute.

We were in the house of the Lord.

But the truth paralyzed me.

I clasped her hand, uttering, "I understand." Removing my clerical robe, I placed it on the altar and accompanied her to the door.

How could I lie to her?

For God and Nothing have a lot in common. You look either one of Them straight in the eye for a second and the immediate effect on the human constitution is the same.[1]

As I drove away, I glanced back at the country church, its dooryard of white gravestones—like salt licks—most inscriptions worn away by time. I thought of the Sundays I stood in its pulpit and prayed for salvation for myself and my parishioners.

The LORD bless thee, and keep thee: The LORD make his face shine upon thee, and be gracious unto thee: The LORD lift up his countenance upon thee, and give thee peace.

Except the Benediction failed to rise to the surface this morning.

And that twilight, alone in my room, I confessed that my appraisal of myself as their revered pastor had been grossly inflated.

Perhaps Ina Gresham had ascertained that truth and lingered behind to shepherd me through the dark passage of self awareness, for my name hung on a placard outside Grace Church's oxblood-red entry doors.

I had replaced its deceased cleric.

Amen, please, Pastor.

In my now pitch-black room I asked the next question:

Who am I, God?

I could have climbed the three steps to that pulpit for years. The babies christened would grow up and marry then return with their spouses to the pews. Catechism classes plus the countless nights

I would have sat vigil at the bedsides of the sick and dying. How often I would have ministered to the troubled in heart and Spirit. And the most humbling task of all: administering the Eucharist where I was most alive in the moment.

Except now it was I who was lost.

The person who I believed I was had up and vacated me that morning in the sanctuary. Even the Bible verses . . . I could recall none save *Jesus wept*.

And what had begun as a moment of panic when no homilies or Bible verses were forthcoming—

When I sought refuge in prayer but was now uncertain to whom or what I was praying—

When I became speechless in the house of the Lord—

Before daybreak in the confines of my room, I witnessed the demise of Pastor Ethan Mueller who had cloaked himself in all the trappings of life everlasting.

I was loath to even look in the mirror at myself for fear I'd be moved to recite the Benediction as he receded into the shadows.

I could no longer inquire in good conscience—*Who am I, God?*

For those were Pastor Mueller's words. No longer mine.

All those beliefs had perished with him.

* * *

From childhood, I'd trusted that I had been created in the image and likeness of God, whose only begotten Son resided in my heart. Now I was its only tenant.

By phone, I asked that my father meet me at the tavern he frequented each morning after he bought the day's newspapers. That Saturday afternoon, I joined him in a booth in the rear of its dimly lit interior.

Forgoing small talk, I told him that I loved him and then came right out with it:

"I no longer know who I am, Papa. It's as if the person you and Mother raised has walked away from me."

He nodded. "Who do you think that person is, Ethan?"

"I don't know. But I've come to say goodbye."

"And the country church parson?"

"He was an imposter. Just as I am."

"Please let Mother know—but not before."

Evincing no emotion, he nodded and, to my surprise, lifted his glass in a gesture as if we were to toast each other. I obliged, and we each broke out in nervous laughter. Then we sat motionless, him staring at the empties before looking up.

"Ethan, I have something to share with you."

I wasn't prepared for what he asked.

"I want you to meet me out at the park, say, around ten tomorrow morning. I won't attempt to talk you out of it, but you owe your mother and me a few additional hours. I need the extra time to prepare."

The Gorge boasted age-old amusement rides, Dodgems, and a wooden roller coaster in addition to a grand pavilion dance hall and several picnic tables, all situated alongside a creek called Big Run. We were to meet at one of those tables.

He held out his hand. "Do I have your word?"

I didn't reply.

"Please," he said. "You'll understand why."

I nodded.

"Cross your heart and . . ."

I grinned, murmuring, ". . . hope to die."

* * *

Prior to falling asleep that night, I reflected on the satisfying moments we'd just spent, asking myself, *Why now?*

At ten o'clock on Sunday, I parked my car and walked through the seasonally boarded-up midway to the stand of giant elm trees and the forlorn picnic tables. With no cloud cover, the sun glanced brilliantly off the creek coursing within a stone's throw. Hatless and wearing a cloth jacket with its zipper open, he sat as if lost in thought. Beside him, a cardboard box with a lid, the kind in which office supplies are stored, and a journal whose leather cover showed signs of wear.

"Thank you," he said.

"For what?"

"Keeping your promise."

I chortled. "Funny, isn't it?"

"She trained you well."

He offered me a cigarette. I refused, gesturing to the box and the journal.

"The *why* of our meeting here this morning," he explained.

I sat facing him as he pulled two faded photographs from his shirt pocket, each of a woman holding a child in her arms. In one she is standing before a towering willow tree with a modest clapboard house in the background and could very well be mistaken for an older aunt because of her matronly dress and the distinct strands of gray hair at her temples. Moreover, the smile playing at her lips is not that of a new mother's delight . . . but nonetheless one of affection. In the second photograph, she is sitting in the passenger side of a 1930s Dodge sedan with its door open wide and the child on her lap who is attired in striped shorts and a matching shirt with, I venture, Buster Brown oxfords and white anklets. The unexpressive gentleman beside her has both hands on the wheel as if he were still driving.

"I know them well," I said.

"Yes, but you were never told who was missing from the photographs."

He stared at me, waiting for my response.

"I'm not understanding," I said.

"Another family member," he replied.

"Of ours?"

He nodded.

Speechless, I felt utterly bewildered.

"Your brother, Ethan."

"Mine?"

Locking eyes with me, and as if ashamed: "Yes."

I stepped away from the table.

"What's his name? Where is he? Why wasn't I told?"

Papa stared at me noncommittally.

"He's dead?"

Overcome by a rush of emotions over a deceased sibling, for a moment I forgot my own tribulations.

He slid the leather journal across the table to me. "You must read this, Ethan. It will only take you a couple minutes. Then we'll talk."

On first glance, it appeared that what I was about to read had been meticulously printed with an ink pen from a finished draft. There were no cross-outs, and the journal's remaining pages were blank.

GREEN LIGHTS IN JELLY JARS (*excerpt*)
by
Christopher Daugherty

The green 1950 Mercury sedan's rear window was festooned with decals of iconic western tourist attractions like the Hoover Dam, Grand Canyon, and Golden Gate Bridge. The car dealer professed its former owner had only desired to attend these places. I purchased the vehicle prior to laws governing the clocking of odometers. This one read an innocent ten thousand miles.

Truthfully, I'd little choice. My car suffered grave transmission problems disguised with a sawdust-and-oil magma. I wagered that the Mercury would travel several hundred more miles than I knew the wounded trade-in could. Whereas, on this humid Saturday in July, the dealer wagered that my Pontiac parked in front of his lot with its cream leather interior and top down would attract an unsuspecting buyer fast.

Driving away, I began to imagine that the Mercury's backseat side windows had once been affixed with gaudy decals too. And would I discover brochures under the seats or in the trunk? Stopping for gas, I noticed that not one tire tread matched and two were vulcanized no-names.

But none of this mattered any longer.

I only needed the vehicle to run until I could paste one more decal on it. Not literally, but in my mind, one that I'd slap over the yellow-and-blue-sky Golden Gate decal.

Mine would be a modest rendering of a skeletal truss bridge spanning the Allegheny just before that river and the Monongahela River joined to form the mighty Ohio. I was driven to discover how many times I could cross it with no headlights after dark, how close on each pass I could steer the car to the bridge's edge without skinning its railing... at what point in one of the passages, I pondered, would the vehicle assume a mind of its own and vault the parapets?

Parked alongside the river that Saturday at dusk, I recall waiting for darkness to envelop downtown Pittsburgh while listening to Stan Kenton perform "Artistry in Rhythm" and "Tenderly" from some ballroom in Ohio, Charlie Parker and Dizzy Gillespie out of Los Angeles, and Johnnie Ray warbling "The Little White Cloud That Cried." That one started me laughing.

Then Chet Baker crooned as if his voice had escaped from a slit throat.

A series of acid-green bulbs encased in jelly jars outlined the bridge's railing. River barges, appearing to be illuminated by the very same lights, moved downstream-upstream.

The dashboard of the Mercury glowed a fiery orange.

When the sky turned pitch-black, I commenced the runs, maneuvering the bedizened-by-wonders-of-the-48 alongside the glowing jars . . . while crooning "Misty."

* * *

I saw my father cry once. That's when Franklin D. Roosevelt died.

It was the only tangible evidence to rely on when I phoned him later that grim night, rousing him out of bed.

"It's me," I said. "Doing something I shouldn't. I can't stop."

Grown-up—probably twenty-six—yet thinking that the next pass was probably going to be my last. Could he detect that over the phone lines? I mean to say, could he smell how frightened I was?

"Where are you, son?"

"Racing back and forth across the Allegheny in a forest-green Mercury with mohair seats, the driver's side now very wet, as am I."

"Hold on, hold on," he kept murmuring.

"Time's up," I said. "Time's up, Dad."

"Wait a minute. Now just a minute. What are you doing on the bridge?"

"Seeing how close I can get to the edge? Have you seen the green lights in jelly jars? Ever tried to skin them without their exploding into a thousand pieces of light?"

Deposit another five cents, please.

Oh, Christ, wasn't that a joke?

"I'm warbling like Chet Baker, explaining to the woman I ain't got another cent in my pocket—*and time's up?*"

I started cracking up when I heard him speak in a measured voice to the operator. "This is an emergency, lady. My number is 7-6208, Sharon exchange. Charge it to me." I could hear him mutter, "My boy's in some kind of distress." She kept repeating, *Five cents, please, deposit another five cents.* "Christ, can't you hear me, lady? Santa Muerte, festooned with green lights, is winging my kid across the dark Allegheny—and they're about to merge with the fucking Ohio! It'll be in all the papers in the morning if you don't let us continue this conversation."

Then nothing.

All we could hear was each other taking air. And for what seemed a whole minute, surely a dime's worth, we breathed heavy, sucked wind, scrambling away from Mr. Taps.

'Cause that's who'd jumped into the passenger's side. Couldn't I see his Alice-blue shoes? The filter tip snuffed out in the puddle of piss on the floorboards? The once-unblemished Mercury I'd coveted for its pock-free chromium bumpers and forest-green paint job, fantasizing that an aging matron had motored in it to the Big Orange, a swain at the wheel singing "Let's Get Lost"?

Jesus, she loved that car. Loved that man.

A trumpet bird whose siren song had lured me over the parapets of the skeletal bridge.

Then I heard my father ask me if I was still there.

"Yes," I said. "Oh, Christ, yes I'm still here."

"Always keep a pocket full of nickels. Promise me, boy?"

"Time's not up," I said.

* * *

Closing the journal, I looked out at Big Run rippling over man-sized ice age boulders in its path. He lit another cigarette.

"It's him," he said. "Westley Mueller. As far as I am aware, he is still very much alive despite my not having seen him for years."

Could I have met him without knowing it?

"He'd fallen out with your mother, who'd begun accusing him early on in high school of taking after me. I did know other women. But to her, life and all its earthly pleasures were to be scorned for the promise of entering the kingdom of heaven at one's passing . . . which, of course, I found totally alien.

"Westley turned on her. Said she was suffocating him in God's name. Then one day he never returned home from school. Not even a note. She suffered no apparent anguish in declaring him dead. 'Better this way,' she kept repeating to herself. And here we are."

I tried to envision my "dead" brother sitting alone at the picnic table closest to Big Run, grinning quizzically at us.

"Was his story fiction? Were you on the other end of the phone line?"

He took a long drag before answering. "He never called me. Westley was sitting at the kitchen table watching the clock before I drove off to work that morning." He laughed at the recollection. "Soon school would start."

"Then how did this journal and . . ." I gestured to the box.

"Came by post a couple of years ago. Addressed to me at the house. Unless someone else sent them, he had to know at least that I was alive and still lived in the house in which he'd been raised."

He placed the journal on top of the container and stood up.

"Find him, Ethan. He's been where you are now . . . Having read much of what's in here . . . I believe it may have been written with you in mind. But stay in the moment as you read. Don't lose sight of your goal. He awaits you, son. However, it will not be revealed to you easily."

Then his customary wry grin. "Unless, of course, you have other plans for later this evening."

Zipping up his mackinaw, he glanced out at Big Run. It was chillier now. The sun had fallen behind the clouds.

"I won't stand in your way."

* * *

Watching him drive off, I reflected how as a child I could barely wait until the picnic lunches at the Gorge were declared over so I could swim in Big Run or climb the ravine to the midway and amusements. I remember sitting sidesaddle with my mother on the carousel's white-and-gold unicorn, a stander and not a jumper like the painted ponies.

Moments later, it was back to the critical decision I'd made earlier. But that was still hours away. Besides, I was intrigued about Christopher Daugherty, who also knew about green lights in jelly jars.

I called back the summer day Mother wore a red polka-dotted shirtwaist dress and aviator sunglasses—Papa's that she had taken from the car's glove box—steering a yellow Dodgem car, me a red one.

As we circled the metal floor amid the acrid odor akin to that of burning fuses, I kept glancing back at her as she gained on me. One more revolution of the arena and we would crash, the impact so hard that my car would be pitched backwards.

Aroused from my reverie by the cawing of crows, I looked up and was certain I saw Papa watching me from the stand of trees. Disoriented, I stood and eyed the tracks of the aging roller coaster. *Would Westley have ridden it with me?* I wondered. *Would he have been terrified of discovering rattlesnakes nesting in one of its seats, as I was? The two boys who jumped to their deaths from the coaster's highest peak upon spotting the snakes—were they my brother's classmates?*

Then I heard children's laughter. But the carousel's painted ponies and white-and-gold unicorn had all been stored for the winter,
as had the Dodgems, kiddie boats, and fire trucks that went round
and round. Even the commissary stand and all its colors of soda
had been shuttered and padlocked.

I glanced back once more at the picnic table.

It sat vacant except for the box of Westley's stories. Perhaps the
joyous cries of past summers' days were coming from inside, now
muted by its fitted lid.

Maybe he is in there too, I mused.

*One day we will meet here to take a dip in Big Run, even if it is
deathly cold. He will rag me for being afraid of rattlers as our front
car in the aging coaster rockets down through the shadowy gorge . . .
and he places his arm around my shoulders.*

It won't feel ice-blue.

CHAPTER TWO

ORIGINS

Carrying the box of stories back to my apartment, I sat down before it that late afternoon, debating if I should begin reading, for I had become obsessed with taking my life like a doomed lover awakened to his fate. Tomorrow wouldn't arrive for me. I'd made peace with that. Yet here before me lay the putative "history" of a brother I'd not known existed. And as dusk turned to darkness that Sunday evening, a faint illumination—similar to that in the bridge's green jelly jars—escaped the box of stories' skewed lid. It was death summoning me in reverse.

Perhaps Westley understood something about staying alive that had failed me. At some point after midnight, I opened the box, and as I read, Monday came and went. Upon completing a story, I'd sit for an extended period, reflecting on it.

On Tuesday, after falling into a deep sleep, I awakened to the arrival of Westley's "Going Dark" manuscript in the mail. Relying on it as a template, since it struck me as his looking-back endeavor, I specifically sought out those early pieces it referenced. It felt as if I were reconstructing him, title by title, in an effort to will him alive.

"The Waffen-SS officers appeared on the screen, twenty feet taller than Papa, in jodhpurs, gleaming boots, and officers' caps with black patent leather bills and silver skull emblems on their crowns. Several wore gold-rimmed glasses. Headlights from their ebony motor cars reflected off the spectacles'

lenses, shooting sparks of phosphorescence across the screen. At that very moment, the real me and the celluloid me coalesced."

YOU LIKE SARDINES? (*excerpt*)

I returned home from school one fall day and found a note on the kitchen table.

Westley, the note said, *ask him what '*Til Death Do Us Part *means. Once I get settled somewhere I'll call you. And take good care of your brother. Love, Mom.*

You're me now, she seemed to be saying. You and he work it out.

When Father came home that evening, I handed him the note, and it was the first time I saw him lose heart.

"What are we going to do?" I said.

"I don't damn well know."

"Who's going to cook and look after Jeremiah?" I asked.

"Me and you, I guess."

"Who's going to wash our clothes?"

"Same," he said.

"Is she ever gonna come back?"

He shrugged, sat down at the kitchen table, lit a cigarette, and stared out the kitchen door over the backyard. It was muddy out there and bleak. The house felt cold and dark. After a while he said, "Whaddya want to eat?"

"I don't know. How 'bout you?"

"You like sardines?"

"Fish?" I said.

"Little ones in mustard. They make good sandwiches."

"I ain't ever tried them," I said.

"Well, let's pretend you and me just went fishing and we pulled these out of Pymatuning Lake. And you can make the Kool-Aid."

So I pulled out a loaf of Wonder Bread and he slathered one piece of bread with yellow stadium mustard and opened the tin of sardines. Laid four headless ones out on mustard bread, then covered them over with a clean white slice. And he cut them in two with a butter knife. Oil and mustard began to bleed through the white bread and out onto the gray speckled Formica. I poured large glasses of cherry Kool-Aid, and we sat across from each other, eating quietly. Kind of like friends. And he smoked. Jeremiah took a peanut butter and jelly outside.

We did this for five nights straight. It was on a Monday that Mother left us. Friday night, he didn't go out. Read the *Hebron Chronicle* in the living room after dinner, then went to bed early. On Saturday after work, he came home and said maybe we should change our menu.

I agreed. Though I had grown to like the sardines, especially when, on the third night, he cut up some onions on them.

"Well," I said, "what can we eat now?"

"Eggs," he said. "Saturday night is a good egg supper night. Go down to the corner and buy a dozen. And get another loaf of bread. We got plenty of margarine she left us, and buy some more Kool-Aid. Any color you want."

When I returned home with the groceries, Father had made up the table real nice. He had dressed it with Mother's hand-embroidered tablecloth, the one she used for Sunday meals. He even had napkins under the silverware and placed a knife inside the spoon on the right side and a fork on the left-hand side of his, Jeremiah's, and my plates like Mother always did.

"We like them scrambled," he said. I thought that was OK, and he began breaking the eggs into a black iron skillet, two at a time, until he had the whole dozen bubbling almost to its rim. He poured in a lot of pepper and salt. And asked me to hand him the ketchup.

"What's that for?" I asked.

"Hell," he answered. "We put it on 'em after; why can't we do it while they're cookin'? Gives 'em color too," he boasted.

That's when Jeremiah noticed he was wearing Mother's apron. And when the eggs were ready, he proudly spooned them onto our plates as if he'd done something real special. He held it out for me as I took a forkful, seeing if they were done to perfection. But the toast had begun to burn, and he dropped the plate of eggs before me and rushed over to the toaster.

Soon we were sitting across from each other again, and it was real pleasant, eating eggs with red veins in them. Then we doused them with even more ketchup and watched the margarine melt into the toast. We drank grape Kool-Aid and were real quiet and enjoying our meal . . . when halfway through, he looked up and said:

"You heard from your mother, Westley?"

I said I hadn't.

"Oh," he said.

Jeremiah had cried the first couple nights. "You seen her, Pap?" he asked.

Father didn't raise his head, but shook it. The moths were beating against our screen door. I told him I'd wash the dishes that night and clean up the kitchen. He seemed appreciative and went in and read the paper. We retired early. And that's the way it went for nearly three months. Sardine sandwiches through the week. Eggs and toast on Saturday evening. Sunday evenings he took Jeremiah and me to Coney Island Lunch, where we each had buttermilk and two chili dogs with everything on, and then went to a movie at the old Paramount Theater. There was always a double feature there, and since it was wartime, most of the movies were about Nazis.

I was glad I was seeing those flicks with him and not Mother. He was our father, and I wasn't afraid the Nazis were going to come and take him away—whereas they might've stabbed Mother with her scissors.

Father came home from work promptly each night, and there were never any mysterious phone calls from women. It was almost as if we were camping out. I'd watched and helped Mother launder clothes, so Mondays became wash days. I hung them in the cellar on clotheslines: his and our shorts, socks, handkerchiefs, bedclothes. He took his white shirts to the Chinaman. On Tuesday evenings I'd iron what I'd washed the day before. (Jeremiah hung around the schoolhouse or played in our neighbors' yards until dark.) Sunday morning—none of us went to church—we shared dusting and vacuuming the house.

"Just in case she ever comes back," he said. "Neither of us can be ashamed."

* * *

"There was this character in my head who owned a basso profundo voice—it could have been Josef Mueller—lecturing me how utterly stupid life was and insisting that to save me hurt and heartache I must 'leap off a trestle bridge,' of which there were several in our town."

RUN HOME, JIMMY MUELLER (*novel excerpt*)

We were studying *Macbeth* in English class when a voice, appearing out of nowhere, asked: *James, why don't you commit suicide on your way home from school tonight?*

Elton Briggs, the teacher, wondered what I thought was so funny. I apologized. "Nothing the rest of the class would understand." But the internal dialogue didn't cease. In fact, this new and strange visitor appeared to have entered my head to pepper me with questions until I conceded I hadn't one satisfactory response to its gloating query: *Why shouldn't you kill yourself?*

The Washington Street Bridge. After school. It's the ideal place from which to leap. Or are you afraid, James? What do you have to live for? Name five reasons that hold you back. One by one I'll refute them all—fucker.

I now walked two people to school and back each day.

Waiting. Waiting. *Are you up for the night?* The voice never slept. If I was in the company of others, it'd step into the background but adamantly reassert itself the first lull in our conversation. Athletics the same. If I was out in right field shagging balls, *This is no fun*, it'd sigh, *and you know it. You're only pretending it's fun to keep me at bay. It's empty bravado, James. Pretend all you want. Laugh and bullshit with your empty friends. Ratchet up the noise. Nothing will work, I assure you. I have all the time in the world—prick.*

Surely one morning I'd awake clear-headed. The voice was preposterous, like one of the crazies who paraded the streets talking angrily to himself.

Why don't you do it now, James? It's the perfect day. One watertight reason why you shouldn't take the challenge, James?

"I enjoy school," I replied. "I want to drive my own car. The powder blue suit in Levine's Haberdashery window will look terrific on me at the senior prom. Rudy Roman and I plan to dazzle our friends in gymnastics assembly next month when we mount a hand-to-hand stand from the reclining position."

The voice replied that not one of these "reasons" was sufficient justification for staying alive. *And you know it . . .* So I stopped going home in the evening by way of the bridge. I walked a mile out of my way by crossing the Jackson Street viaduct instead. It hung closer to the Neshannock. If I went over the side, perhaps I could swim to shore. But in the morning, so as not to be late for school, I took the Washington Street Bridge. Racing across it at considerable speed, I'd warble a love song at the top of my lungs while the voice droned:

Just a matter of time, James. Just a matter of time.

And Jeremiah hadn't a clue.

* * *

The reference to Jeremiah at first both puzzled and embittered me. *Had Mother given birth to yet another child?* But, anguished by that possibility, I chose to believe that Westley, being their only child, had simply invented Jeremiah's existence. I, too, had an imaginary brother who became an integral part of my early years, especially at night as we awaited sleep, transfixed by a passing car's headlights racing across our walls.

PART TWO

CHAPTER THREE

THE QUEST

It was apparent that Papa knew more about Westley than he was telling me. He'd chosen to let the stories speak for themselves, suggesting that he believed they were more revealing than my brother ever had been when they lived under the same roof.

Apparently we had two paternal uncles: Stephen, a monsignor in the Roman Catholic Church, and Felix, who had spent the bulk of his life in traveling carnivals and circuses, performing a variety of roles, including a Joey, a trapeze artist, and a faux hermaphrodite in the Ten-in-One, or freak show. The brothers reappear in the stories in various guises.

I, however, had grown up believing I had one surrogate relative, "Aunt Ruth," my mother's closest friend, and that my grandparents had succumbed prior to my birth.

Westley was manifestly preoccupied with the contrasting careers of our uncles. He depicted our devoutly religious grandmother as attending mass daily to pray for them, whereas our grandfather, who earned his living as an ironworker, erecting trestle bridges over the many streams and rivers that flowed through and around Hebron, preferred the saloon over a kneeling bench. The pair resided in a single-room tenancy on the south side of town alongside the railroad tracks and the tin mill.

Early on in their marriage, our parents had moved to a better neighborhood of Hebron, set on raising a family not haunted by the ill-conceived hopes, poverty, and mayhem that for generations had characterized their kinfolk's lives. Papa, who had once served as an altar boy during high mass, even joined the new neighborhood's Protestant church with Mother and for several years taught a men's Sunday School class prior to abandoning religion altogether.

But sometime around my brother's tenth year, the scourge of fatalism from which they had tried to escape began to reassert itself.

It's this and successive years that Westley writes about as if to release himself from their memory.

* * *

I continued to spend each day reading, followed by a very unsettled sleep, roiled by much of what I'd learned, especially how utterly superficial my own life had been.

By that, I mean I envied my brother's passion, his deep hurt, and the conflict he encountered—willing to stay alive and not succumb to our mother's death wish. Yet by the time I came around, that wish had been heavily veiled, as if it had all been transcribed in anguished passages and then secreted deep inside her heart. I only knew her as God-fearing, consumed by the expectation that I would not fail her as Westley had, and would accept the Man of Sorrows as my savior.

I freely obliged. All of my life's choices were predicated on that commitment. I never questioned the countless scriptural teachings she shared with me nor what I learned in church, since that would have been heresy. Each night before turning in, I recited the Lord's Prayer and slept soundly. My future had been spelled out for me, and I rested in inviolable confidence that I'd be justly rewarded in the afterlife.

Even Papa, the nonbeliever, looked upon me with a soupçon of pride. I suspected my parents at some ineffable level hoped that they had finally broken from their past. Yes, my brother was "dead," to their way of thinking, but I had obliged my mother's deepest longing to atone for all of her and my father's mortal shortcomings. I was preparing to devote my life ministering to others in His name.

Except I envied Westley's stories.

What were mine but paeans to the Father of Abraham for sacrificing his only begotten Son God in my behalf, acknowledging I had or would commit an egregious wrong? Why had I penned such anodynes, basking in the compliments of my elders?

But Westley early on knew who he was . . . or perhaps it's more correct to say he knew what he wasn't. And each night after reading, his presence virtually hovered above those onionskin manuscript pages.

If only he would utter my name, I believed, then I would have a reason even at this late age *to be somebody*. *To exist*. Yes, I was alive to others, but only as an imposter, an actor.

Exactly what Christopher Daugherty had written in "Going Dark."

* * *

There were one hundred and twelve story manuscripts and two unfinished novels under Westley's pen name in that box. I estimated that just shy of a hundred had been published over a period of fifteen years. And after several days of virtually nonstop reading of the complete oeuvre, I began again, this time taking notes in an effort to provide clues as to his possible whereabouts.

I refused to consider the possibility that he was dead.

In one piece he'd quoted Anaïs Nin: "We write to taste life twice." Westley, I trusted, wrote also to disgorge it by some fanciful alchemy in an effort to release its grip on him. Yet in story after story the reader quickly observes that the effort is futile, and the familiar narrative reappears again and again in various disguises.

All told, there were a dozen or more stories that comprised the core of his work.

So I sought to explore where I might pick up his trail. I was now guardedly optimistic because his work evidenced an indomitable will to survive. Why else would he have kept turning over the stones of his life? The "Going Dark" tale manifests a protean self, an identity that found no ballast in multiple personas, yet perseveres as if their composite may amount to one.

In an early tale of his, Westley gave me ample reason to set out to find him. I record its initial paragraphs.

* * *

MASQUERADING AS A REVOLUTIONARY
(*excerpt*)

Leonard's father, brother Felix, and he vowed early on to get out of town. His mother and sisters had no such ambition. "Perfectly fine for us under the willow tree in our backyard."

"We want Gotham instead," the men said.

Mr. Hart never made it. Following a deathbed request, Leonard took the bus to Geneva-on-the-Lake, Ohio, where the family spent one week each summer. He walked to the water's edge, said a brief prayer, and shook his father free of the black funerary urn.

It was empty.

Mrs. Hart and Leonard's sisters had salted him under the willow tree.

Even more determined to escape Hebron—"You'll perish here," Mr. Hart prophesied—Felix borrowed his father's sedan one Sunday afternoon. Its carburetor burst into flames on a country road, as did Felix, who trotted across a wheat field, dripping fire. "That's one way of getting out," Leonard mused.

They sprinkled young Felix under the willow tree, too.

One summer night before his senior year in high school, Leonard waited until his sisters and mother were sound asleep before waltzing out of the house. His Schwinn bicycle was stationed against the willow tree. Carrying only a change of clothes in a pillow case, he knelt.

"Pap, Felix—I'll come home for you someday. Keep the faith." He embraced the tree.

Anguished over his departure, Mrs. Hart traveled to nearby towns on weekends and spoke to merchants in an effort to track down her son. A neighbor, two years after the incident, swore she'd seen him standing on his head atop a golden palomino in a Mills Brothers circus over in Meadville. That same week, another said her daughter had seen him playing drums in a cocktail lounge at Conneaut Lake Park.

Leonard, over time, was spotted singing with Stan Kenton's band in Cleveland's Starlight Ballroom; as an extra in *From Here to Eternity*; on a Pennzoil racing team at the Indianapolis 500. Then, one Christmas Eve, the local butcher told Mrs. Hart her son was a missionary in Havana, Cuba.

"How are you sure, Mr. Prioletti?"

"Che Guevara and the Holy Mother appeared to me in my dreams last night. It's Leonard—the priest masquerading as a revolutionary."

But Leonard Hart was holed up in a single-room tenancy on 114th Street in Manhattan, one block off Broadway and near Columbia University. He worked replenishing shelves in a Times Square bookstore, and periodically sold his blood to make ends meet—five dollars for the first pint, seven dollars thereafter. Only once had he encountered someone he knew from Hebron—Gertrude Eckstrom, his high school drama coach. Engrossed in reading a copy of *Billboard*, she'd taken a seat opposite him at the Horn and Hardart Automat. Leonard fled, leaving his soup and Parker House rolls untouched.

His attire he acquired at a Goodwill thrift shop on East 57th Street. Preferring Brooks Brothers suits, he owned one chalk-striped blue serge and a cocoa-brown three-piece worsted. His recycled shoes were cordovan, and he saved a vintage forties camel-hair topcoat for special occasions. The closet in his SRO was not much larger than a broom stand.

"At least I've made it to Manhattan," he thought, and did avail himself of its art museums, especially the Frick; the public library reading room on 42nd Street; and an occasional subway ride to Greenwich Village. There he'd sit in the corner of the White Horse Tavern and read Thomas Wolfe, his Chesterfield draped over an empty café chair.

When Columbia was in session, Leonard attended the Saturday night socials sponsored by the university YWCA for its unattached women. A shot of scotch at the West End Bar on Broadway (the ghosts of Merton, Ginsberg, Kerouac, and Lucien Carr pettifogged in the corner booth) helped gel his courage to approach a stranger. To an uncritical eye, Leonard Hart in the blue serge and bluchers looked as if he might be the scion of an upper-class family, residents of the Mystic coastline . . .

* * *

The uncles'—Stephen and Felix—repeated appearance confirmed Westley's preoccupation with those professed opposites. In one story the main character is the barker outside the midway's Ten-in-One, and then several narratives later, he reappears in a cowl of undyed wool. Westley penned exacting descriptions of the contrasting pageantry and rites in which each man engaged. Moreover, no one story featured the influence of one uncle to the absolute exclusion of the other. Where this all led, I wasn't certain, but I had no reason to believe that when he wasn't writing, his absorption with these diverse life styles and commitment would cease.

But the excerpt from "Masquerading as a Revolutionary" offered an address of sorts, one far beyond our birthplace of Hebron. Reference to the infamous West End Bar near Columbia University had occurred elsewhere. He described bookstore employment and an attraction to wearing secondhand bespoke suits. It was a paltry assemblage of evidence to set out on, but the prospect of encountering my *raison d'être* in a sibling I never knew existed yet who understood the import of little green lights in jelly jars on bridge parapets . . . was, for the time being, adequate to dispel my five-days-earlier dark resolve.

I boarded an express Greyhound bus to New York City late that Saturday evening.

CHAPTER FOUR

NEW YORK CITY

Crossing the Pennsylvania Turnpike in a torrential downfall, I thought about the many nights as a boy when lying in my bed I'd turn to *my* imaginary brother and talk until sleep came. With him I could be myself and not fear retribution for having failed to live up to the impossible. But come morning I rarely sought his presence as long as I was around others. It was easier being a true believer in the daylight.

Yet here I was on an urgent quest to seek out my actual brother when it struck me: *Were Westley's stories his way of saying, "Find me, Ethan"? What had he learned about me? And why had he sent them back home if he knew our father seldom opened a book to read?*

The rain never let up over that long bus ride, plus I hadn't slept. Arriving at daybreak at the Port Authority complex, I now surmised that Westley and I were in fact looking for each other . . . but not for the same ends.

* * *

HOTEL RIVERSIDE SUITES (*excerpt*)

The room had one window, a metal cot, a lime-green chest of drawers, and a mirror that hung on the backside of the shellacked door. The distance between the bureau and the bed was the width of a heavyset man. Twelve pairs of shoes placed toe to heel, its length.

Each morning an attendant in an electric-blue cotton uniform knocked. Did he want his bed made?

Muller always said no.

A portable Royal typewriter sat on the bureau alongside a comb and a straight razor.

Tenants stole each other's rations. Over the weeks of his stay, he cinched his belt tighter, taking secret pleasure in returning to the weight he'd held as a young man. On his trips to the single-room occupancy's bathroom, he'd open the bare communal refrigerator and laugh to himself. A second mirror.

It'd been one week since the trace of onion juice and ground meat had all but disappeared from his clothes. But so had most of the wages he'd earned on the grill. When hunger began to threaten his concentration, he'd lie down upon the cot, look up at the cracked ceiling, and visualize lemon meringue pie—the White Tower specialty. Methodically he'd cut himself a wedge and then, savoring each bite, even the ceiling crumbs, he'd devour the memory.

The lunch surfeit would carry him through to the evening meal at Horn and Hardart. These latter days, it consisted of a serving of Parker House rolls and a glass of milk. He'd pocket packets of sugar cubes to melt in a hot-water drink for bedtime.

Muller had no clock. The thread from morning to half-light or darkness was the clacking of his typewriter. After dressing and splashing cold water on his face each dawn, he'd lift the instrument off the bureau, pull the window blind down so that the room was in virtual blackness, and sit on the bed to begin working with his back against the wall.

He typed for hours, interrupted only by the ceiling repast. When his output was niggardly, he'd punish himself.

"I can't look at the pastry," he'd cry, staring vacantly into the darkness. Even the sugar tea was off limits.

Muller had no idea what he was writing, for that was the presumption. "If I know what I'm about to compose, then what is its value?" Better to absent oneself as the machine clacked, one page of text followed by another, all hammered onto the white rice paper in darkness. Prior to turning in each night, he'd gather the pages in sequence and resist reading them under the overhead light.

Actually, there was somebody else inside his room.

A genius of a writer, Muller believed—for whom he was the designated medium.

"Talk to me," he'd urge. "I'll get it all down."

In the early days of their tenancy, it would take hours for the guest to break his reticence. As noontime approached—bodies shuffled in the hallway, a sign they were traveling to the empty refrigerator—Muller grew increasingly anxious. The Riverside Suites tenants passing his door in midafternoon could hear him utter, "Please."

* * *

Westley had roomed in Riverside Suites while working midnight to 8:00 a.m. at various White Tower establishments as a short-order cook. He'd return to the room, sleep for a few hours, then write until it was time to return to work. It was all recorded in "Hotel Riverside Suites."

But the SRO no longer existed.

After a full day wandering about the neighborhood, I returned to my hotel that evening and began to seriously question what it was I hoped to discover. Did I honestly believe that by some stroke of good fortune I'd meet someone who knew him? I had visited the West End, nursing a couple of bourbons . . . but why?

You could have put your time to a more rational use by lying in bed and staring at the lemon meringue pie on the ceiling, I mused.

Moreover, even if I truly believed Westley wished to establish contact with me, he would not make it easy. If I was unable to demonstrate a high degree of single-mindedness and imagination to seek him out, I'd be of no use to him. His stories made that clear. The quest was, in essence, a test for me.

There was a gentleman seated two tables away from mine, reading my every move, whom I guessed was about Westley's age yet bore no physical resemblance to anyone in our family, but what did that mean? I decided that I'd return to the West End the following day. If he was there, I'd approach, saying I was looking for my brother, Westley Mueller. "You wouldn't happen to know him, would you?"

Then I ceased to get carried away.

Was I writing his stories?

That night, I began sorting the manuscripts according to where they took place and ascertained that New York City figured prominently. One told of a father taking his fifteen-year-old son to Manhattan by train from a small burg in Pennsylvania, describing how they dropped coins in little glass compartments to eat at the automat, before climbing a flight of stairs off Broadway to taxi-dance with Gotham women in their embrace.

That had to be Westley and our father.

Visiting a club in Greenwich Village, they were joined at their table by two young women. The father bought drinks, announcing, "We're staying at the Statler," and coaxed the less attractive of the pair to "Cozy up to my young friend." The boy recoiled when she clutched his thigh under the tablecloth, hoarsely whispering, "You got the looks to be in show business, honey."

The narrative concluded in the hotel room with the father chastising him for "wimping out on a night you'd never forget. You come to New York City to grow up, son!" Except the boy assumed he had, by witnessing two men in drag dupe his father. Yet he *was* smitten by the "show business" remark.

If this had truly happened to Westley, I begrudged him the experience, having enjoyed no such introductions to manhood. Were the pair more like two friends than like father and son?

Or was it Westley's way of explaining what had gone on before me, suggesting that I shouldn't lament what I'd ostensibly missed?

* * *

It's as if he's letting me know what it would have been like if I'd been there.

As I lay in bed with the manuscripts strewn about and listened to a roomer talking to himself as he lumbered past my door to the only bathroom on the floor, an unsettling thought caused me to get up and begin pacing the floor. In an effort to ignore it, I began counting the windows in the apartment building facing my hotel.

But, like a neon sign in a derelict saloon, *What if,* it flashed, *you were in fact the other little man?* I shuddered at the notion.

Maybe Westley did have a younger brother . . . and it was you, Ethan.

All those references in the stories to Jeremiah?

The prospect was so disturbing that I became nauseous.

And the voice in my head bantered:

It's the meringue pie.

In a state of dread mirroring the night his persona drove back and forth across the bridge, each pass within a hair's breadth of grazing the acid-green lights in jelly jars, I began trembling. The hotel room had no telephone. But who would I call? And what would he tell me this time when I said that I might be the Jeremiah in Westley's stories?

"Is there any truth to that, Papa? For Chrissake, you must tell me. Were you not man enough to say? Is that why I'm seeking out my brother, one I never knew existed—*or did I?*—to help me back?

"And back from where, Papa?

"Did I stand on a stool in front of a four-way mirror in the haberdashery and be fitted like Westley for an Easter suit? Did Westley and I share a bed all those years?"

I stepped out into the hallway and found the lavatory door unlocked. Inside, I bent over the porcelain toilet and began heaving, all the time holding one hand under the running faucet, trying to get a grip on myself.

Your imagination is getting the best of you, Ethan. Straighten up. There is nothing wrong with you.

I stood up, splashed cold water on my face, and glanced in the mirror, which had lost much of its silver backing. Shards of my face. But it was enough to help settle me.

I had no idea who Jeremiah was. He was Westley's imaginary brother.

How could he be me?

And I began laughing, mocking my reflection: "Jesus Christ, Ethan, you've been so engrossed in your sibling's yarns that you're damn well getting lost inside them. Where do you think you are? In that room in Riverside Suites?"

I could not let myself be sucked into the vortex of unreality.

Westley had struggled with that.

CHAPTER FIVE

REVELATION?

Cajoling sleep, I lay back down and concentrated on lights from the street chasing each other across the ceiling. A radio played across the hall. Its dial was being spun, and the discordant sounds complemented the illuminations overhead. But then the roomer settled on a Billie Holiday recording of "Don't Explain."

I thought about Westley's story of the father-son pilgrimage to Manhattan and the boy's heralding "the most incredible music" emanating from a 52nd Street jazz club called Birdland. I turned on the light and began rifling through the manuscripts on and about the bed. Somewhere in the pages, Westley, as an adult, had revisited that scene in some detail.

I located the passage in a lengthy work that I took to be an unfinished novel.

As if he'd lost his way.

By now, Lady Day was caroling "Willow Weep for Me." The volume cranked up as if she stood outside my doorway.

* * *

NOVEL EXCERPT

At his urging we walked up to 52nd Street, "The Street of Jazz," and paid the cover to a downstairs club called Birdland.

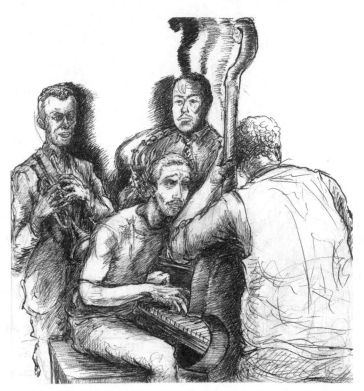

"There's Bird," he whispered. Charlie Parker was the mythical jazzman he couldn't quite believe ever existed anyplace except inside one's head. Charles Mingus was on double bass, Bud Powell at the piano, and a young trumpet player, Miles Davis—all on the stand.

A dwarfish black man introduced the group. Bird, for some mysterious reason, grew belligerent and began harassing the announcer, tauntingly calling him "Shorty," while the target of his mockery hollered from the back of the room for Bird to "get on with the damn set." Whereupon the saxophonist seized the stand-alone microphone and pitched it out into the audience . . . before he began to blow.

We couldn't take our eyes off Powell, who soloed with his eyes closed. The pianist struck a simple melody that, at first, repeated itself in single-voice hornlike lines mildly embroidered at different octaves. When he introduced a driving left-hand chord accompaniment, it seemed as if the Steinway grand would levitate. The tempo of the notes had ratcheted up, and the lines had become so extended and harmonically complex that the once simple refrain of "You Go to My Head" had been transformed into a raging dialogue only Bud Powell could "sing."

Then the room fell nearly silent—no other sound whatsoever except the drone of the club's air handler. The players, with their eyes shut and their heads resting on their chests, were concentrating on Powell cascading through the tune's chord changes—*but he wasn't actually playing*. He continued soloing, except he wasn't. His fingers flew over the keyboard—but never lit on any of the ivories. The lines were all occurring inside his head, and he was "singing." Straining, we could hear a high-pitched nasal drone. His fellow musicians periodically broke out in wide grins.

* * *

"Let's check out Harlem," Mr. Willard exclaimed as we exited Birdland. He flashed Billy a wide grin as if he knew what was on my friend's mind.

We rode the A train to 125th Street and found it as bustlingly alive as downtown Manhattan. Nearby, tucked inside a hotel, was an intimate jazz club called Minton's Playhouse. On the bandstand, a musician wearing a beret, horn-rimmed glasses, and a goatee and holding a bent-bell trumpet intoned a scat phrase over and over.

"I can't believe it," Mr. Willard whispered, transfixed.

The place was packed with white and colored folks, and many of them accompanied the Diz under their breaths as he chanted his "Salt Peanuts" tune . . . and then, as he began blowing, they bobbed to the rapid beat of the radically different, undanceable "new jazz" whose melody became the stepping-off place for each musician's improvised score . . .

Behind Gillespie and his quintet stood a giant mural of four jazzmen—guitarist, drummer, trumpeter, and clarinetist—alongside a woman in a red dress lying facedown on a bed. Our friend, whose mood quickly mellowed, had been eyeing it closely.

"Honor, that be Lady Day up there in that brass bed sleepin' off a drunk. She break your heart so bad when she sings 'Fine and Mellow,' you understand why love is same as a faucet. You able to turn it off and on."

Next day we took the subway to the south pier to catch a glimpse out in New York Harbor of Miss Liberty, looking resplendent in the morning sun.

"Jesus Christ, she's green!" our friend crowed.

Yet when I read what immediately followed, everything else of his seemed to pale in comparison. Sleep would not come easily.

That very night after we turned in at a seedy hotel off the Bowery, I waited until Billy and Mr. Willard had settled in, then slipped out of the room and descended the three urine-scented flights to the dank lobby. When we'd entered earlier, I could see right off that some rooms weren't used for sleeping. A sign at the check-in desk advertised ACCOMMODATIONS BY THE HOUR.

A willowy brunette, her magenta lipstick a dramatic foil to her milky cast, sat in a dark corner, impassively smoking a cigarillo; her legs were crossed, one of them counting out seconds.

I slid alongside her.

After taking a studied drag, she icily remarked, "I don't do wemen, honey."

"How did you know?" I asked, surprised by more than just her odd pronunciation.

"Men ogle you from where they squirrel their conscience. Where's yours?"

I shrugged. "I guess in here," I said, pointing to my heart.

"Ain't where a man packs his."

As hard as I tried, I could never get Billy's swagger down, even when I felt as hard as nails.

"What are you doing here?" she asked.

Before long, I was talking to her as if we'd met long ago in the notch-ery back on DeForest Road. She kept nodding as if nothing I said was the least unfamiliar.

"Well, I seen you eyeing me when you came in earlier. There must be something you want from me, honey . . . or you wouldn't be sitting here."

I told her.

Within moments she was up and alerting the man behind the cage. "Solly, if one of them comes in looking for me, tell 'em to wait right over there. I'll only be a minute."

Her room, at the end of the shadowy hall on the first floor, consisted of a narrow bed, a full-body mirror on wheels, and one rust-stained porcelain sink mounted on a wall. The window was covered with a poster of a nude Marilyn Monroe posing on red velvet.

Then her closet, half the size of the cell-like room.

What surprised me was how meticulously ordered it was. There were compartments for socks, scarves, blouses, sweaters, panties and bras. Dresses of all colors and fabrics were neatly hung with the hangers all hooking in one direction. There were hats, too, maybe a dozen stacked neatly on top of each other.

"It's the costume shop. The naughty stuff's in there." A tall metal locker stood at one end.

"Don't take too long, sweetheart. Say, what *is* your name?"

"Honor," I said.

"Oh Jesus, honey, they'd pay you extra for that," she sighed, closing the door behind her.

I knew exactly what to do. There was something very arousing about undressing before her mirror. Standing across from Marilyn staring at me . . . seeing what kind of *wemen* I was going to be. When I slipped on her panties, they had a fragrance of violet sachet about them . . . I immediately saw Alsada smiling at me from over by the door. Nodding, she was. Like *Yes, do it, Honor. We all got to do it at some point. And don't you feel wonderful? Don't you feel like a woman? Ain't it something, girl, to feel like a woman?*

I slipped on the brassiere and again stood this way then that in front of the mirror. And placed my hands on my now-covered breasts and began sobbing as if someone had returned to me, as if these were hers and not Honor's. The woman looked out of the mirror at me, extending her arms, and pulled me to her and kissed me softly.

Oh Christ, yes, I was holding myself and crying like a damn baby in Alsada's arms, Miss Emma's arms, and my absent mother's arms—wherever she was—coming home to me; this woman, rising up inside me, and now I reached out and saw a black dress that somehow I felt I'd once worn. Don't know where. But once a long time ago I'd had it on and a man came over to me, called me by my name, holding out his hand, and asked me to dance.

"You look so fine in that pretty little dress," he said. "Why, it barely covers your dimpled knees."

And I started laughing.

"Oh yes," I said, and spun coquettishly around and said, "Will you zip up the back, sir?" Like he was actually there.

Then slipped back onto the bed and rolled her black hose up my white legs and prayed to God that those shoes with the rhinestone stars, the ones with the shiny black heels, would fit.

And yes, they did, a bit tight.

But that was no problem.

'Cause I no longer had to walk like a man.

Then I heard her softly knocking, whispering, "I'll be needing the room in a minute or two, Honor. Hurry."

"I'm ready," I said.

I opened the door and my friend stood there, admiring me. "Praise Lazarus," she sang. "If I wasn't the kind of lady I am, I'd take you over any old damn man. What a stunner!"

She spun me about and zipped up the dress.

"Are my seams straight?" I asked.

* * *

On my initial reading I'd never given much thought to the narrator's recounting outfitting herself in a scarlet woman's garments. *But that person was Westley.* And it speaks of a yearning, the quality of which I couldn't recall encountering in any of his stories.

Now it was past midnight and I was fully awake.

Was there a message about myself in these particular passages?

Was Westley revealing even a darker truth to me? I again began poring over my notes and the manuscripts. And then remembered . . .

* * *

I NEED A WOMAN

She hadn't been gone but two days. One might have expected a whimper of grief, like "Christ, I miss her. What am I going to do alone?" I climbed out of bed and opened the door. He was standing naked in our hallway.

"Go back to bed." I pulled the blind so the neighbors wouldn't see.

"You don't understand," he cried. "Her dresses. Her shoes. The toiletries on the bureau. Her undergarments in our chiffonier."

Now, at the fall interval of his life, *his* dam had ruptured—brought on by Mother's death. Here's my father unable to sleep because he's blubbering, "I need a woman!" What the hell was I going to tell him?

"Do you understand what I'm talking about, son?"

"Well . . ." I said.

"You just don't get it. Come here." We stood outside their bedroom. "Go in there and pull open the top drawer of the chiffonier."

The room was dark save for the streetlight laying an amber puddle across the bed—one side slept-in.

"Go on, open it."

Inside, neatly piled, were panties, camisoles and slips, and—bunched in one corner—a cluster of brassieres. The drawer let loose a breath of sachet.

"That's what I'm talking about," he said. "Now, open the closet door. Go on, do it, James."

Plaid knife-pleated skirts, georgette shifts, crêpe de chine empire dresses, blazers, all draped on wire hangers; mules, espadrilles, and spaghetti-strap heels assembled underneath. On the upper shelf—black pillbox hats whose veils she'd let fall at weddings or funerals. On his side, prosaic two-piece suits in summer and winter blends. The closet was redolent of gardenia.

"Do you get it yet, boy?"

He ambled down the stairs.

"No damn way are we ever going to get rid of her presence. You can throw all that shit outside, clean every nook and cranny of her belongings, toss out the creams and face lotions, the prescription bottles, her

Bible, her photograph, you name it. Scour her out of every board and plaster in this house, and she still won't leave."

I poured us coffee.

"*I need a woman*," he whispered, his face a hairbreadth from mine.

"I don't get it, Pap. What are you telling me?"

"You really want to know?"

"This isn't like you."

"Do you grasp why she wore those things up there? That smoky sundress with jasmine flowers, for instance? She'd stand there admiring herself in the mirror, watching me button it up her backside. Those peekaboo nets she'd drop over her china-blue eyes? Undergarments the shade of her blush?"

"Why?"

"*So I wouldn't have to wear them.*"

"Yeah, I get it," I said. The damn whiskey was blubbering.

"Listen to what I'm telling you. *It's your mother's stain . . .*"

"Finish your coffee so we can go back to bed."

"No. You don't get it!" he bellowed, bounding out of his chair. A gingham napkin from the buffet drawer was tied under his chin—a babushka. Like she might have done, he pressed his face on mine, and, *sotto voce*, mewled again, "*I need a woman.*"

I followed him up the stairs.

We entered the darkened room, and in a fury Father snatched her garments out of the closet, the chiffonier, the bureau drawer—heaping everything onto the bed they had shared for decades. With each item, his frenzy accelerated. The last garment on the clothes pole, a navy-blue button-down-the-front frock with a stiff sailor's collar, he held up to his torso. "How about this, Junior, with my patent leather *please-fuck-me* shoes? Are my seams straight?" He turned as I'd witnessed her do many times, bending a calf up toward his derriere while staring over a bare shoulder.

The streetlight's corrugated shade serrated the room's shadows. With one swipe he pitched the bureau's opaque perfume bottles and pearly emollient jars across the floor and under the bed, a chromium lipstick tube the lone survivor. He opened it and studied himself in the mirror, my face his double.

Was he going to paint both our lips?

"Pap, please, stop this absurdity."

"I've no bosom!" he cried. "My chest is a goddamned void. Look at me!" A salmon brassiere dangled from his neck. The circle he'd drawn around his mouth exaggerated our pathos.

"What's left for me, James? Will she ever come home?"

Father lay down upon her wrappings, burying himself.

Grief.

Causes people to do the strangest things. His was implacable. I still had him. Her departure hurt, but I could abide it. Yet a piece of him was half gone. It was as if the heart was now eating itself in some kind of bizarre, comical remorse.

I slept downstairs that evening.

At first light, I softly opened his door. Their room had been restored. He was sound asleep. His frozen magenta "O" faintly smudged.

* * *

"So I wouldn't have to wear them."

Westley's narratives actually spoke to his yearning for a single identity and had no more to do with finding that place in a woman's body or her clothes than in the various male characters in which the narrator found life. The father in "I Need a Woman" aches for that which has been taken from him—his opposite, the woman who each day confirmed his identity as a male. Now, only her garments testify to that and are powerless to alleviate his loss; and so, as if to bury himself, he puts them on.

Once again it harked back to "Going Dark."

This was my eureka moment.

* * *

Quiet out in the hallway now. Even the lights from the street had muted on my ceiling, their movement lethargic now, not erratic.

I gathered the manuscripts, placing them at the foot of my bed.

In a strange way, it felt as if at least the penumbra of my brother had joined me in the room, for earlier, I'd truly had no notion of who he was.

Now, I'd begun to comprehend that he hadn't either.

I, too, had been somebody once. I thought about the tale of a man too cowardly to kill himself, so he believed he was dead.

Was that what Westley was up to?

Fading off to sleep, I even speculated he'd become Proteus-like out of necessity, as no single persona is adequate for any one of us.

CHAPTER SIX

SHIFTING IN AND OUT OF CHARACTER

Unable to rid my mind of ceiling pie, the next morning I slipped two quarters into an automat's glass window display and sat down to eat in the crowded dining area with other menfolk looking just like me—a vagrant.

Except now I didn't feel as lost.

Westley Mueller was many people, moving in and out of characters either by will or because of the circumstances of the narrative forcing him there. And it dawned on me that the information I was piecing together wasn't so much to inform me *where* he was but *why* we should meet. That *why*, I chanced, is that our lives were bound by an inextricable fate.

In effect, we had met on the bridge of acid-green lights in jelly jars.

My quest would succeed only if I was able to discern that the *why* of our impending meeting was for each of our sakes . . . and not mine alone.

I looked around, curious whether he'd caught my eye.

I'll find you, brother, I mouthed. *Watch me. I will find you.*

And this time the meringue pie will be on me . . . and not the ceiling.

Exiting the automat, I eyed the tops of fabled buildings—the Chrysler and Empire State—and women, their nails polished cinnabar, passing sylph-like in spiked heels, a breath of an alien perfume in their path.

It was now *our* quest. As if I were the fabled brother, Jeremiah, about whom he had written so much and whom he'd slept alongside all those boyhood years. Except I knew I wasn't.

Did it matter?

If he had been shadowing me back in the automat, he was now at its window, grinning wide.

* * *

Perhaps I overstate Westley's conflicting identities. But to consider his principal characters as a means of finding him made more sense than, say, searching for him in Gotham.

What immediately came to mind was Papa's brothers: the priest and the clown.

* * *

SHE'S A LITTLE STORE INSIDE (*excerpt*)

My father, Jacob Müller, had three siblings. Stephen, the monsignor; Felix, who doubled as a clown and lion trainer for the Mills Brothers Circus; and sister Eva, who sold her body until it shook too much.

When it came time in Jacob's life to sum it all up, to prepare himself for what might or might not occur after death, he didn't knock on the sacristy door. Instead he sought out Eva and Felix, who lived in run-down bungalows on the outskirts of our town.

As a boy I couldn't understand why.

I loved frequenting Uncle Stephen's cathedral with its flying buttresses, its west and east stone towers, one carrying the great bell, the other housing more than one thousand pipes for the electro-pneumatic organ in the baptistery. Monsignor ascended the grand circular staircase in his polychromatic chasuble at high mass while racks of ruby-red, ink-blue, and clear votive jars bearing flame and melted wax illuminated wooden saints, and morning sunlight filtered through stained glass clerestory windows. And there on the rood screen separating the choir from the nave, a crucifix larger than the statue of Franklin Delano Roosevelt on our village green—Christ's gold-leafed body, mirroring the votive flames. Alive.

Parishioners rising and crossing themselves, kneeling, rising again . . . their solemn incantation echoing Uncle's Latin liturgy.

And Christ on fire.

Why a whore and a clown? I wondered, when Monsignor Stephen owned a golden ring with a giant ruby that his congregants kissed.

"I'm off to the whiskey bar," Father said. I clandestinely followed to see if the monsignor would embrace him in an alleyway minus his surplice and the two of them would stroll into the backdoor of the parish house.

Instead I watched Father walk wide of the large shadows that the basilica towers, Temperance and Perseverance, cast across Main Street like an ominous embrace.

* * *

Aunt Eva sat in the shadows of her porch on summer afternoons. A Kewpie doll with rouged cheeks, and henna-dyed hair that haloed a china face. Her dress dropped inches above her bony knees. She wore spiked heels painted with fuchsia nail polish and dreamily stared onto the dirt street, her slight body jerking as if a motor oscillated under its bottom. Waiting. Waiting for a blanket of darkness to eclipse the bungalow.

I asked Father what Aunt Eva was selling, since so many men stopped by after dusk.

"She's a little store inside," he said.

Once, as I was passing her house, she signaled me over.

"I'm your Aunt Eva," she said. "You look exactly like Jacob."

"Pleased to meet you," I said.

"Your father chooses to ignore I'm his sister."

I nodded as if I understood.

"You must come by and visit me sometime. We'll get to know each other better." She grinned.

In time I learned what she'd been selling inside her bungalow. That she took off her gaudy doll clothes for strange men. Then I dreamed of paying her a call. I envisioned her standing disrobed in her bedroom, arms outstretched to the door jambs, one foot touching the other, and the henna triangle burning like the bush in the Bible. A smoke of yearning curling out of Uncle Stephen's censer.

Her image provoking the ache I bore for the gold-leafed crucifix.

But as Aunt Eva's tremors grew more conspicuous over time and the traffic upon her walkway diminished . . . so did my ardor and contrition.

Her house was no longer freshly painted a periwinkle blue. Its front steps fell into disrepair. Like a plaster-of-Paris palmist inside a cloudy glass arcade box, she sat staring out her window. You place a nickel into a slot, her wooden hand overturns a queen of spades, and a cardboard fortune drops out—somewhere, you imagine, below her skirts.

Except a house fly had died on her forehead. Flesh-tinted plaster exposed chalky stigmata. These women in arcade boxes are saints too, I thought. Lesser saints than those mutely lining St. Margaret's side aisles. Or Christ pinioned against the rood screen—He was the master saint, the biggest and best of all the arcade ones, and of those who lived on dirt streets like Aunt Eva, waiting, waiting, for acolytes with jingle in their trousers.

* * *

Uncle Felix lived one street over from Eva's place. He kept a palomino in a shed behind his modest one-story house. On Independence Day, he dressed like Tom Mix and headed a parade down Main Street with paper American flags attached to his steed's halter. He'd painted stars on its hooves and braided its flaxen tail with red and blue ribbon. A large, barrel-chested man with chiseled features, Uncle Felix resembled an American Indian.

"He could whup lions!" a bystander exclaimed. "Make 'em lie down docile before him like house tabbies."

Felix Müller swept his Stetson against the sweaty flanks of his golden horse.

"I seen him standin' on the back of a galloping Arabian once," said another, "a pair a six-shooters blasting crockery out of the sky that clowns spiraled aloft like barn swallows."

"Was he a trapeze artist too?"

"If one of those spangled dames dangled by her gams—you bet! He didn't join the circus to get away from 'em."

As the parishioners glowed, watching Monsignor Stephen's vestments sweep the basilica's cobbled floor, the Eucharist chalice ascending to the giant rood, so, too, did the town's women in Uncle Felix's wake. Always he'd spot a comely bystander, dismount, and, like the gentleman I think he never was, boost her onto the horse's backside. The pair would clop up the pavers past Hutton's Hardware, the Episcopal church, and the post office, halting before the viewing stand, where Uncle Stephen officiated alongside the mayor and chief of police.

Felix's woman gripping his midriff, the horse perspiring under her thighs.

The two brothers locked into each other's gaze.

A splinter of wistfulness marred the cleric's severe demeanor. *The bouquet of incense is impotent to satisfy a man's need to scent a woman*, he sighed. *Felix feels the drumming of her heart, her hot breath against his neck*. And for a single blasphemous second, he envisioned her splayed against the basilica's apse, a thousand votive candle flames rising up to illuminate her. Stephen blinked, removed his steel-rimmed frames, and rubbed his eyes, praying the image that returned would be the worthy one.

But she mouthed his name, beckoning for him to veil her nakedness with his peacock robes.

His malicious brother, Felix, taunting him about women when really all he ever yearned for was salvation.

Felix flashed a sardonic grin, gesturing to the weighty crucifix that hung about his brother's neck.

"He suffered a big letdown, too, Steve."

PART THREE

CHAPTER SEVEN

THE WINDOW HARP

Now, when Westley looked at himself in the mirror, he saw me lurking in the shadows, and the priest and the clown knew why.

The references were too many to be ignored.

I returned to his story "The Window Harp," in which Peter, the young narrator, gifts a silver ring with a Sacred Heart crest to Jeremiah, his kid brother. Early on, it was sent to their father by his sibling in the hope of influencing the eldest boy to follow in the cleric's footsteps. Peter speaks of having taken comfort in the gift especially when he was feeling "vulnerable."

Wouldn't that experience be compounded if one was having difficulty finding an identity to which one could claim title?

So I began to wonder if my brother might have followed in the footsteps of the mysterious monsignor uncle he never met.

And if he had, the irony that each of us had committed to serve God in some higher capacity—surely to save ourselves—was affecting. Could he have entered the priesthood? Was he still active in the faith, or had he, like me, abandoned it?

* * *

St. Boniface Seminary of Sewickley had been established in the 1850s by a Benedictine monk to serve the Pittsburgh diocese in preparing candidates for the clergy. With the pretext that I was compiling information on a deceased relative, I made an appointment to visit.

"It's an effort for the benefit of his surviving brother—my father," said my appeal.

I was introduced by a Father Hinchey, a dour prelate in his seventies, to a lay staff woman who had assembled a folder with numerous photographs of Stephen A. Mueller, his high school transcript from our hometown of Hebron, and various articles he'd written for the seminary's biweekly newspaper. Poring over the material in St. Boniface's library and taking notes in the expectation of sharing them with Westley when we finally met, I was surprised to learn that he had been a tennis star and won numerous trophies in a league of East Coast theological schools.

Thanking the secretary, a kindly woman attired in an unornamented, liturgical-blue dress that contrasted severely with her coiffed, feathery white hair, I said I'd one more favor to ask of her.

Father Hinchey had excused himself much earlier.

"I've a boyhood friend of whom I've sadly lost track for a couple decades now. I recall how enamored he was of the mass while growing up and often when we were together alone in either his house or mine"—I hesitated, and began to laugh in a self-deprecating manner—"we'd play priest."

"Oh?" she said, uncertain as to what might follow.

"Yes. We'd set up an altar and place the Host on a plate—God forgive us—and, dressing in sheets and paper miters for the occasion, mime the Eucharist. We took ourselves quite seriously and never intended our actions to be blasphemous, mind you. One time he would be the priest and I'd be the altar boy. Then next occasion we'd switch.

"Occasionally his little brother would wander into our service, and we'd appoint him as the parishioner who had come forth to partake in the bread and the wine."

She held her pale fingers against her lips as if in shock but couldn't disguise a suppressed grin.

"Well, I beg your forgiveness, but this is all a prelude to inquiring if my dear friend ended up here at some point in his life."

"I'm a bit surprised you both didn't," she countered. "What's his name?"

"Christopher Daugherty."

In essence, Westley Mueller, upon leaving home, had been declared dead. Moreover, he wouldn't have wanted to be traced. I guessed he may have persuaded the authorities to permit him use of a pseudonym—perhaps, say, the one he later used in crafting his stories.

She said that she'd search the archives covering the years in question.

Watching her return shortly with a bound ledger, I was hopeful, except her mien suggested otherwise.

"There is no Christopher Daugherty, I'm sorry to say."

"All the possible years?" I asked.

"Yes."

I rose to leave, thanking her, and handed her Uncle Stephen's folder.

"But there is this," she said, opening the register and pointing to a photograph of one J. Ethan Daugherty.

"Could he possibly be related to your friend?"

Ethan Daugherty, in wire-rimmed glasses, had glistening dark hair combed back and wore a thin-lipped smile that could easily have been a smirk. The eyes, luminous, and ruddy angular face aped Papa's and mine. Despite my never having seen him in person or happened upon his photograph, I felt I'd known how he looked from childhood.

But why had he taken my birth name?

Flustered as to how to respond, I muttered, "He's my friend's kid brother. The one who partook in our Eucharist offering."

By now Miss Vincent and I had become allies. "I've got grown sons myself," she said, "who once loved taking up the collection from assembled family members in baskets they'd jury-rigged to look like those used at St. James."

"Do you suppose I could borrow this overnight?" I asked. "I'll return it to you in the morning."

"Please. Father Hinchey I don't think would approve."

"You have my word."

* * *

That evening, I sat opposite the open yearbook, euphoric that he was in fact real, for I had been haunted by the dread that he never was.

That perhaps all the stories I'd read were in truth mine.

And I'd forwarded them home in an effort to save myself. A consciousness deeper than my own wasn't prepared to call it quits . . . so it was acting in its own self-interest.

Anything is possible, I thought, sitting across from Westley. *Except it's undeniably you. You followed Uncle Stephen to St. Boniface.*

* * *

The following morning, Miss Vincent and I perused the material she'd assembled on J. Ethan Daugherty. Not surprisingly, he, like our uncle before him, had been the captain of St. Boniface's tennis team. In our section of town, tennis was viewed as an upper-class sport. Yet, outfitted in tennis whites, Westley stared unflinchingly at the camera. I also learned that upon being ordained, his initial placement was the Sacred Heart parish in Pittsburgh's East End.

"The diocese office should be able to help you," she offered.

I promised Miss Vincent I'd drop her a line if I located Christopher.

But something troubled me: the uppermost buttons of his tennis shirt were undone, and a fine chain bearing a man's ring adorned Westley's neck.

* * *

THE WINDOW HARP (*excerpt*)

He kept eyeing me while opening the box, uncertain whether I was teasing him.

It was a container I'd borrowed from Mother's jewelry drawer. Inside lay a silver ring.

"But why? It belongs to you, Westley."

"No longer," I said.

The ring had been sent along with several religious texts to our father years earlier from a younger brother who'd entered the priesthood. A note instructed Papa, "Pass these on to your eldest in the hope that someday he will choose to follow in his uncle's path." The ring had etched on its face a crimson Sacred Heart and Uncle's initials, S. M.

On days when I felt especially vulnerable, I wore the ring about my neck, often not understanding why. I prayed that Father Stanley Raymond Mueller was protecting me.

I threaded the chain through the ring and placed it over Jeremiah's head.

"I wear it for you, Westley. For you looking out for me."

That's when Mother came through the door with empty arms. "Is your father home?"

We shook our heads.

As if she knew better than to inquire, she climbed the stairway and closed their bedroom door behind her.

Jeremiah folded our theater. I blew out the candles. We followed her up the stairs to our room on the other side of the hallway.

From our window, our backyard creek—it originated at the old stone quarry up our road—refracted the moonlight to ripple across the ceiling above our bed. We didn't dare fall asleep until we were certain she had.

Perhaps a half hour had passed when we heard the doorknob turn and her shuffle barefoot out into the hallway.

The hallway window looked out onto Widow Colucca's house. We could hear Mother put her face to the glass. It's what she often did when in distress, as if the glass were her cage. She would hum or moan into it, creating a kind of a glass harmonium.

A sound that terrified us to our core.

And once she started to slur with her watery lips, Jeremiah grabbed my hand.

Then the window music ceased.

She shuffled—it sounded like dance steps of her own choreography—to our door.

We could hear her heavy breathing against it.

Jeremiah clutched Father Raymond's ring.

"Good-bye," she whispered. "I'm off now, boys. Westley, always remember what I told you. You are your brother's conscience. Don't try to follow me. I know my way."

She paused. A stifled sob rose from deep inside her. Then silence. We could picture her composing herself.

"When he comes home . . . you tell him."

* * *

Cement Dam was up our road a distance in what is now the woods. Our county once intended to divert the meandering Big Run River through the flatlands, where they constructed a towering dam to create large camping and fishing grounds that would attract folks from as far away as Cleveland and Pittsburgh. There'd be a huge open-air dance pavilion that would feature famous bands every summer weekend.

Except Big Run continues to flow in its centuries-old path, while the dam sits mysteriously deep in the forest like some mythic wall, inviting the sick at heart and feeble of mind to plunge from it to their deaths, mostly around religious holidays.

Jeremiah kept sobbing into my chest. "Momma, please don't."

And then we heard her pad down the stairway.

Waiting until the kitchen door slammed shut, we opened ours. From that hallway window—death's musical instrument—we could see her handprints on the upper pane, then spotted her between our house and the widow's; she was ambling nude past her rosebushes and lilac tree out into the street.

Her pace quickened as she headed up toward the quarry.

* * *

Back in my rented room, I sat staring blankly out the window, conflicted by having spotted the Sacred Heart ring. Years after that photograph of Westley in tennis whites was taken, the narrator of "The Window Harp" had gifted it to his younger brother.

Who, of course, would be me.

Was he not looking out for me in my absence?

Then from "The Window Harp" I read aloud the following:

Jeremiah, like our phantom uncle, entered the seminary upon graduating from high school and for nearly a dozen years served a working-class parish outside Pittsburgh while I taught high school English in a couple of East Coast preparatory schools. On the few occasions we saw each other, I never broached my suspicion about his not being truly wedded to the clergy. We'd laugh a bit, nervously recalling a dark incident or two of our childhood but seldom more. Mostly it was small talk. Despite my effort to defer to him more often than I naturally might, at some level I sensed Jeremiah still suspected I was playing the role of the older brother and seeing through him.

So I wasn't all that surprised when I received a phone call from him late one winter night and, after tentative greetings . . . he ceased speaking.

What I heard on the other end of the line was the hallway window glass harmonium. "What is it, Jeremiah?" I cried, struck with the fear of that recollection. "What's going on?"

"Mother's come back," he said.

"She's dead."

"No, Christ no. *Can't you hear her?* She's handed me those crocheted undies we used to fuck with in our Punch and Judy skits. We're headed out, Ethan, to you-know-where."

I lived several hundred miles away. Nuns from a nearby convent would periodically look in on him and tend to his spartan needs in the parish house.

"Are you alone, Jeremiah?"

"I'm sorry, Ethan. But the body of Christ tastes like stale Wonder Bread. His blood—rancid Welch's. And my soul is more foreboding than our bedroom when she would stand outside it, taunting us with death. Making us savor it . . . to lift it up like the heavenly host to our Westinghouse bed lamp. Well, she's returned in all her naked glory. Good-bye, dear brother."

The phone line went dead.

By the time I was able to get somebody to enter the parish house, he'd disappeared.

Having just returned from St. Boniface, I felt the parallels couldn't be more revealing. Westley joined the priesthood, became an assistant pastor at the Sacred Heart in Pittsburgh's East End, was assigned to other parishes over several years, and then dropped out. Jeremiah, the kid-brother persona, uncannily mirrored *me*.

Jeremiah and I had shared the same bed for eighteen years. There was no hiding the truth, even in a darkened room that overlooked a creek whose water eventually flowed into the magnificent Ohio.

Even though I was more cowardly than he, I was convinced much of his bravado was mere bluster to disguise his having to look up to his older brother. There were instances when he became truly frightened and sought my assurance that everything was going to be okay. I was as frightened as he, but swore that it would pass. In effect, we lied to each other and were under no illusions that we hadn't.

The distressing truth is that Jeremiah was *alive*—yet I wasn't.

A veritable construct of her piety and fear of living, I, Ethan, was the embodiment of our mother. But I preferred Westley's, for Jeremiah and he were constrained to explain the window harp's nocturnal plaint that accompanied her demoniac choreography outside their bedroom door.

How could they not lie to each other to save themselves?

Yet as a child I swore never to prevaricate, nor to despair. And the nights that I awoke inchoately fretful, I called upon God to ask *Why?*

Now I envied Jeremiah's life, his relationship to Westley.

At times I felt as if I were squirreling my way into his stories so that I might discover myself.

CHAPTER EIGHT

NOTEBOOK FOR ANNA MAGDALENA BACH

Records at Father J. Ethan Daugherty's last pastorate, St. Vitus in New Kensington, Pennsylvania, indicated that he'd abruptly departed. Was there speculation as to why he'd left? Most of those with whom I spoke weren't puzzled by it at all. "We have little say. The diocese decides."

A secretary within the parish office gently reminded me that over two decades had transpired. "I didn't know him." But she directed me to a parishioner who might be of some help: Elizabeth Andrews, a widow and a faithful member of St. Vitus for years.

I phoned, explaining that Father Daugherty was an acquaintance and that I hoped to meet up with him again.

At first Ms. Andrews seemed chary of confirming anything more than yes, she remembered him. When I pressed for greater detail, she asked, "How well did you know him?" Once I indicated that we'd grown up together in the town of Hebron and had been the closest of friends, she began to open up, recalling his conducting high mass. "How precise he was, his sacerdotal attire, the manner in which he approached the sacrament of the altar, the sweeping of the censer—all of it spoke to an ecclesiastical choreography of his own design. He performed as if it were a dance for our Holy Father."

Lost himself within the ritual, I mused.

"Did the parishioners like him?"

"Despite an apparent aloofness, he was actually a very caring priest. They were quite fond of him and felt bewildered when he left."

"Do you know why he did?"

She offered a curt "No."

Our conversation looked to have come to an abrupt close.

"Please don't take offense at what I am about to ask you, Miss Andrews," I said.

"Of course not." Her tone was more circumspect now.

"Was there another?"

"*Another?*"

"A parishioner."

Once again . . . dead air.

"Apologies. I mean to inquire if, say, his involvement with a member of the church might have led to his leaving of his own volition . . . a lady, perhaps."

"I saw no such evidence," she quipped. "Why do you ask?"

I could have ended the conversation there, but her discreet manner, and now benign curiosity, allowed me to continue.

"He's my brother," I whispered conspiratorially.

"Oh, I didn't know he had one."

I refrained from agreeing.

"Perhaps you would like to talk in person?" she said. "I live close to the parish house. Why don't you stop by?"

"Now?"

"Yes, of course."

She was standing in her open doorway when I approached the clotted-cream Victorian's ample porch.

I was struck by her austere yet youthful presence, having expected a much older woman. Lithe in frame and attired in a plain white smock, the Turneresque silk scarf that tied her russet hair in a tight bun was her only concession to adornment. Her radiant mien and penetrating gaze caught me off guard.

Extending her hand, she appeared momentarily confused, looking through me almost.

"Ethan Mueller," I said. "Pleased to make your acquaintance."

"Yes," she answered, as if as an afterthought, and turned into the living room, which felt overwhelmed by a Steinway grand. We sat in facing Queen Anne chairs upholstered in coral peonies. The light from the late afternoon was diffused ochre because of the cloth blinds pulled halfway down the windowpanes. It bled stream-like across the massive lid of the mahogany piano.

She answered my gazing at the instrument. "This is my teaching room," she said. "I have students most every afternoon, a few of whom are exceptional . . . causing that lovely instrument and me to be very accommodating."

"He sat there on certain afternoons, didn't he?"

"Yes." She grinned, eyeing me as if she expected me to say something more. "It's why I invited you in . . ." There was a moment of expectant silence. "Ethan."

Another being expressed a longing for him that touched mine.

Sensing my difficulty, she shook her head and confirmed again, "I honestly don't know where he is."

We sat mutely in the embracing warmth of that room as unassuming as she. I could almost hear the afternoon lessons being played out each half hour of every weekday afternoon—a rare few inspiring.

I gave her an attenuated version of my story: how Father Daugherty was my brother yet I'd never met him, let alone known that he even existed.

And as the minutes turned into nearly an hour—it was a Saturday afternoon—it became apparent to me that Westley had sat in this very room sharing his story, for nothing appeared to surprise her regarding mine.

Elizabeth had this habit of bending her head in thought while clasping her hands together and turning her fingers over each other, a continual caressing of sorts. When conversation ceased, either hers or mine, she would look up and glance straight into my eyes.

Was she seeking my brother?

It was clear that the intensity of the conversation, particularly the way I expressed myself, had begun to take its emotional toll on her. I'd not spoken to anyone so openly as I had to her, not even to my father.

Somewhat ashamed of myself, I stood and said I had to be going.

Elizabeth reached up and motioned for me to sit back down. "For a moment," she pleaded.

As we sat facing each other again, it felt as if she were trying to awaken a memory in me. *Or was I fearing that?* After a moment, she stood and, from a small stack of piano books on the Steinway, lifted one with a yellow cover, handing it to me.

"Your brother's."

It was the *Notebook for Anna Magdalena Bach*, piano compositions.

"Each Wednesday at three o'clock, he sat here. That was his lesson book."

"And he played?"

"Quite beautifully," she replied.

She had given me yet another piece of him. There had been no musical instrument in our house. Leafing through the compositions for "young players," I checked the margins for jottings, possibly his. A sixteen-bar exercise, "Aria," listed its due date in red pencil: Feb. 2nd.

"Your brother loved the Minuet in G Major," she said, and began playing. The piece was unfamiliar to me but exceedingly lovely. I envisioned Westley performing it as a child with her at his side. She turned to me, smiling wistfully, and I began to hum the melody as if it were as familiar to me as my face.

At its last note, the hush in Elizabeth Andrews's music room lingered. A shard of late-afternoon light illuminated her hands at rest on the ivory keys. Her eyes closed in private reverie.

For reasons unknown to me, I was suddenly overcome by a wave of anguish. I cannot explain it in any other manner except to say that at that moment, I could not help believing that I had once sat beside this comely woman in this very same room, and the longing to reawaken that suppressed memory haunted me terribly. Or was I merely yearning to have been beside this russet-haired beauty of deep intelligence and restraint as Father Daugherty once had? Was I reading her longing for his presence and willing it to mine? Had they once been intimate?

While self-consciously murmuring about having to leave, I stood and walked to the door before looking back. She was standing at the Steinway.

"Tell him I miss him, Ethan," she said softly.

"If I find him," I replied.

"Oh, you will."

And as I pulled open the door, she called out:

"You asked if there had been a woman."

"Yes," I said, somewhat startled.

"I believed he yearned for one deeply. When I described how he choreographed the mass?"

"Yes?"

"I always felt that it wasn't Christ so much that he wished to embrace but someone more palpably real . . . one whose warm breath might grace his touch as he elevated the silver cup high into the nave."

Then I knew.

"Do you think he understood that?" I asked.

Elizabeth hesitated before responding, turning her fingers over each other. "No. One day he surely would."

A chaste and unrequited star-crossed longing had sought expression through the Anna Magdalena Bach exercises each Wednesday afternoon at three.

* * *

When I pulled Elizabeth's door behind me that day, the time with her augured an unhappy end to my quest.

Maybe it's wiser to go on about my way, I mused.

It was apparent to me by now that the price one had to pay to become closer to him might be higher than I could afford. My green-lights-in-jelly-jars moment had brought me to the lowest point in my life; I didn't ever want to go back there, but I worried that I might have to as the stipulation to embrace my brother.

When I arrived back at my room that evening, I returned Westley's stories to the fiberboard box in which they had been mailed.

I wanted time away from him . . . from myself.

In the morning I'd decide how I was to move forward.

* * *

But at some point in the night, I awakened with a start . . . or that's how I mentally recorded it at that time. Sitting up in bed, I observed how the traffic outside my window seemed unusually heavy at that hour. In fact, it felt as if cars were passing by at considerable speed—numbers of them. I lifted the window blind and discovered that I was standing on the shoulder of a highway. Ahead rose a gigantic trestle bridge, one with red lights on its highest girders to alert low-flying aircraft.

I turned back to return to my bed, but nothing was there except a steep precipice adjacent to the roadway. I began walking toward the bridge as the vehicles continued to zoom by, and it was then that I spotted the acid-green jelly-jar lights. They illuminated the bridge railings every several feet.

Curiously, I found myself comforted by them even though I have always had a deathly fear of heights and panic always set in when crossing a bridge, whether by car or by foot. Yet in this instance the lights seemed familiar to me. As if I had been here before. *I know this place*, I thought. *There is nothing to be afraid of.* I began to move to the center of the bridge. The sound of the river below now began to drown out the sound of the heavy traffic . . . nearly as if it no longer existed.

I looked back once again to confirm that I was alone. Were my bed, my window, the house no longer there for certain? And that's when I spotted my car parked on the roadside. Its headlights were still on. But it was the Mercury sedan I'd owned while attending seminary.

Then it came to me: yes, I'd been here. It was the night of my spiritual crisis.

The night I had turned my back on God and all that I had ever believed in. It was the night that I'd realized how terribly alone I was. The night I'd felt as if I had been abandoned by my very own soul, and I was nothing more than an empty vessel driving my car to nowhere. I'd stopped on this bridge.

Recalling that, I began to chortle.

First it was God who evaporated.

And now I was uncertain whether I was in fact real and not the ephemeral substance of my own dream.

For there seemed to be no beginning or end. There was nothing to return to. Where did this road lead?

* * *

I started cracking up when I heard him speak in a measured voice to the operator. "This is an emergency, lady. My number is 7-6208, Sharon exchange. Charge it to me." I could hear him mutter, "My boy's in some kind of distress." She kept repeating, *Five cents, please, deposit another five cents.* "Christ, can't you hear me, lady? Santa Muerte, festooned with green lights, is winging my kid across the dark Allegheny—and they're about to merge with the fucking Ohio! It'll be in all the papers in the morning if you don't let us continue this conversation."

Then nothing.

All we could hear was each other taking air. And for what seemed a whole minute, surely a dime's worth, we breathed heavy, sucked wind, scrambling away from Mr. Taps.

'Cause that's who'd jumped into the passenger's side. Couldn't I see his Alice-blue shoes? The filter tip snuffed out in the puddle of piss on the floorboards? The once-unblemished Mercury I'd coveted for its pock-free chromium bumpers and forest-green paint job, fantasizing an aging matron had motored to the Big Orange, a swain at the wheel singing "Let's Get Lost."

Jesus, she loved that car. Loved that man.

A trumpet bird whose siren song had lured me over the parapets of the skeletal bridge.

Then I heard my father ask me if I was still there.

"Yes," I said. "Oh, Christ, yes I'm still here."

"Always keep a pocket full of nickels. Promise me, boy?"

"Time's not up," I said.

* * *

"Where are you calling from?" he asked.

"Pittsburgh. One of its many bridges."

I could hear him rustling, perhaps turning on the light to check the time.

"Why, Ethan?"

"Because nothing's changed."

Why was I phoning him at this late hour? I wondered. *What was the implacable need to hear his voice? Was it the child in me wanting him to watch me high-dive? So he could huzzah? Marvel at my form? Yet there are no lights on the rivers this night, the mighty Allegheny or the Monongahela as they merge to coitus in the grand Ohio.*

Perhaps that was why I called you, dear Father.

Perhaps you could be waiting for me at the confluence, and then together we will stroke through the night out to sea.

"You've been quiet," he said. "Let me hear you speak, son. What are you thinking?"

"*Thinking?* Oh, I've stopped doing that. I keep returning to this place."

"Cold out there tonight? Are you dressed warmly? It rained here all day today. And what about the traffic? Many cars on the road, son?"

"Mine with the parking lights on several feet away and the motor running."

"Radio on?"

"What?"

"What's playing, Ethan?"

"''Round Midnight.'"

He laughed. I did too.

"I have some news for you. A bit of serendipity that you phoned..."

I didn't respond.

"Are you still there?"

"Yes."

"Your brother called."

I couldn't believe what I was hearing.

"Ethan?"

"I'm here."

"Had very little to say. When I answered the phone, it seemed as if nobody was on the line, except I could hear breathing. At first I thought it was you and kept calling your name. Finally he spoke. It was a terse '*Westley. It's Westley.*'

"'*Where are you?*' I asked.

"No response.

"I told him I missed him.

"'*Could we meet somewhere?*' I asked.

"Silence.

"'*You know your mother passed away, right?*'

"'*I do,*' he said.

"Please come home, son."

"Are you speaking to me?" I said.

"Of course. Of course I am speaking to you."

"I'm sorry to have awakened you, Papa."

"'Round midnight," he jested.

"'Round midnight," I echoed, placing the receiver back in its cradle.

At that moment I no longer could hear the sounds of the river nor the cars rushing by. In fact, I found myself standing at my window with the blind never having been raised. I returned to bed and, in an effort to understand what had just transpired, realized that the time I'd spent earlier with Elizabeth Andrews had had a much stronger effect on me than I'd thought.

Yet the moments on the bridge and the conversation with my father seemed so real that I couldn't convince myself that it had all been a dream. *Could I have phoned him from here?* I wondered.

The receiver felt cold to the touch.

Almost as if he had taken its trembling orb into his calloused hands, held it up to his lips, and murmured *'round midnight* over and over as if those words meant something. But what did the heart care except to be held and spoken to?

* * *

Within a month of my visit with Elizabeth Andrews, I had a teaching position in an inner-city high school where most of the students were African American. Virtually all of us who taught there, including the administrators, were white.

Listening to my students' stories, I reflected on the egregious amount of effort and time I'd expended on my own stories; as each week passed, the bridge incident's pernicious hold on me was diminishing. Westley and his whereabouts no longer occupied my every waking hour either. I rested in the conviction that he would approve of my self-control and the need to sort out all that I'd learned.

It was during that first summer recess, sometime in mid-July, that I received an envelope with Elizabeth's return address. Inside was a handwritten note appended to a postcard.

Dear Ethan,

It had fully slipped my memory when we shared that lovely after-noon together becoming acquainted. And it wasn't until I was clean-ing out my very messy desk last week that I came upon the enclosed. It was, as you will see, addressed to me with no greeting or salutation therein. The date, barely legible, looks like it was posted about four years or so after Father Mueller left St. Vitus parish.

My deepest apologies for not recalling it sooner.

With affection,

Elizabeth

The postcard was a washed-out black-and-white photograph of a cowl-attired monk herding sheep on a hillside meadow. Dark clouds threatened rain. I could tell the address was in his hand-writing because of the sparse notes he had appended to several of his stories.

The inscription below the photograph: *Holy Cross Abbey, Ber-ryville, Virginia.*

Of course she hadn't forgotten receiving it. She'd withheld the postcard from me because of his having won her promise to honor his desire for total privacy. I suspect no one even knew of his tak-ing lessons from her. I pictured him entering through the alleyway that abutted her back porch, he in street clothes, no less, incognito. He was an "actor," after all. Their moments together—maternal, platonic, of course, but shot through with untrammeled openness and revelations. Elizabeth was affording me an attenuated look in-side what she certainly knew and understood about Westley. It is no wonder the mass had become a theatrical piece, a *pas seul*, when he presided.

But over the months following our meeting, it had obviously anguished her to receive a clue as to his possible whereabouts. And at the risk of betraying him, she forwarded it to me, I suspect in the hope that she knew him well enough, expressed through the *Note-book for Anna Magdalena Bach* lessons, to be sure that he would forgive her.

Perhaps she didn't want me to abandon my quest, to write the story that he, Westley, hadn't yet composed.

PART FOUR

CHAPTER NINE

THE MIDWAY AND THE MONASTERY

MONKS

"Don't be fooled by what you see," he cautioned. "Like anyplace else, there are a lot of *pricks* here."

Formerly a landscape architect in Boston (now his eighteenth year in the order), Brother Paul had a stuttering problem. So severe that he'd steadfastly grab onto something solid—a leg of a table, say—while he agonizingly spoke. And perchance out of a sense of the diabolical, he would lock you into his gaze, daring you to turn away, when these seizures occurred.

"*P-P-P-P-Pricks*," he spat.

I assumed one had committed him to the odious detail of guest master. You might have thought someone welcomed it. The guesthouse was heated and had hot and cold running water, a real kitchen, and soft chairs. The only remnants of the barren monastic life in this house were his straw bed—disguised with a fitted sheet—a dark cowl, and the cross he bore to entertain pilgrims like myself.

In the monk's barnlike domicile there was only cold water, piped to a communal bathing stall. Several showerheads hung inside what looked like a milk house with its concrete floor and cinder-block walls. Each day shortly after 3:00 a.m., the monks would rise in their unheated four-by-eight stalls that were separated by six-foot-high walls and appointed with a mat of straw on a wooden platform, one blanket, a straight-backed chair, and a clothes hook; the openings to these stalls had no coverings.

With the abbot positioned outside their cubicles to accompany them in the morning prayer, the monks, stripped to the waist, would repeatedly lash the knotted ropes, the *disciplines*, across their backs until recitation ceased, followed by the communal bath at 3:45 a.m. The showers in the wintertime were left half-running to prevent the water from freezing. Then back into their cowls and on to matins.

Adjacent to the barn domicile sat several outside toilet sheds.

While Arthur was off praying, I sat alone with Brother Paul in the guesthouse living room. Responding to his earlier caveat, I asked, "Brother, why should you have to suffer such vindictiveness in a monastery, of all places? Do God's will beyond these gates."

Brother Paul clutched his hands together and began stammering. His azure eyes appeared chinked with bright amber.

"I would be frightened to death out there," he replied.

And said no more.

I visited the monastery library, a conference hall off their sanctuary with very high ceilings and hundreds of books lining each of the four walls, towering nearly ten feet or so on sagging pine shelves. The volumes weren't Dewey-decimalized or, for that matter, organized at all. An exegesis text on the book of Luke would be shelved next to the *Institutes* of Calvin. Or *The Jews from Cyrus to Herod* would be resting alongside Karl Barth's *Christ and Adam*. Greek, Latin, and a few Hebraic texts—all mingled together. In the empty room's center sat several tables pushed together with metal chairs haphazardly placed around them. The monks retired at 7:00 p.m. Instructions and the reading of religious texts occurred from 9:30 in the morning until 11:45, prior to lunch. The remainder of the afternoon, physical labor or choir duties followed. When I asked Brother Paul how learned most of these monks actually were, he smiled.

He had spent untold hours studying alone in this library and countless others more catholic. In vain I sought works of fiction, believing I might at least find a copy of *A Portrait of the Artist as a Young Man* among these shelves. I did come across a few old parochial-school readers and a copy of *Gray's Anatomy*.

* * *

Prior to departing on Sunday at noon, Arthur introduced me to the abbot during the official visiting hour. I was inclined to share with him that my uncle Raymond was a monsignor and director of the diocese's Society for the Propagation of the Faith, but I thought better of it. The three of us wandered down to the outbuilding where the monks slept. As we entered their quarters and walked past the open stalls, the abbot hesitated in front of one, turned, and gestured into its interior. The stall was like all the others, just as I have described: a straw mat on boards, a chair, a cowl suspended from a hook . . . and I haven't mentioned a container of holy water (now frozen) roughly nailed to the partition. But lined against the shared partition wall and piled on crude wooden crates stood a dozen or more plaster of Paris figures painted in garish colors— all saints—several sparkling with fake gold dust.

The abbot looked vaguely annoyed . . . his cross to bear, I presume. The stall belonged to Brother Stanislaus, an octogenarian from Bavaria, barely articulate in our language and virtually senile.

"Our exception to the Order," he volunteered.

Past the dribbling showers in the converted milk house and out again onto the barren, snow-covered field, he inquired if I would like to see the library.

"No, Father," I answered.

I hoped I might catch the old monk returning from wherever he had gone. In a broken tongue, perhaps he would identify each of his plaster of Paris figures for me. How apt, I thought, Brother Stanislaus alone here in a snow-covered Virginia cornfield among his sole possessions, Kewpie-doll saints and a sackcloth habit, the weight guesser of this hallowed carnival.

When I bid good-bye to Brother Paul, I looked deep into his eyes, then at the stump he'd begun to mold his hands into, and essayed to speak the tongue of Trappist monks—

The tongue of silence.

Paul, don't let the pricks destroy you . . . Life might have been so much better with you on the outside.

Except we knew it was just another lie. Besides, he'd placed a pound of butter in my jacket pocket while Arthur, buried deep in thought, shadowed him up toward the gate and our Ford.

* * *

Elizabeth Andrews's alert had caused me to recall one of his earliest stories in which we're told of a winter retreat that he and his friend Andrew had made. But rereading it, I was struck by the absence of any compelling mystery the monks engendered in the writer. What did stand out was his heartfelt admiration for Brother Paul, the guest master, and his fascination with the Brother Stanislaus persona. The estranged old monk from Bavaria ignited Westley's imagination, even if the monastic community itself didn't.

"The weight guesser of this hallowed carnival."

Within that character's clouded mind and his gilded plaster of Paris dolls lay the ineluctable mystery of God, it seemed.

And with a pound of butter in his coat pocket, my brother exited the monastery's gate. I read Brother Paul's gesture as Westley's underscoring the sublime fatuity of his three-day encounter.

* * *

Westley was actively forcing me to read the ambiguities. In seeking him out, I was unavoidably becoming a person I had never been.

If I had read Elizabeth's postcard as a direct, unequivocal clue as to where his persona had taken refuge, "Oh, please," he might have ragged. "Concentrate."

As if those acid-green lights in jelly jars hadn't presaged something more ominous.

Or the sound of the window harp.

* * *

I hoped I might catch the old monk returning from wherever he had gone. In a broken tongue, perhaps he would identify each of his plaster of Paris figures for me. How apt, I thought, Brother Stanislaus alone here in a snow-covered Virginia cornfield among his sole possessions, Kewpie-doll saints and a sackcloth habit, the weight guesser of this hallowed carnival.

The image of Brother Stanislaus and his gussied-up saints had pierced the stifling uniformity of the order for Westley. Yet casting him as the "weight guesser of this hallowed carnival" stymied me.

What was in his mind?

Among the stories was one, "To Swallow His Heart," depicting the narrator's Uncle Felix, who had left town as a young man to join the circus, and who had obviously left a strong impression on the young author's psyche.

It portended that I would not happen upon Westley at the Berryville monastery or any other for that matter.

We would meet at the carnival.

* * *

TO SWALLOW HIS HEART (*excerpt*)

Earlier at the carnival's gate, he'd reached into his pants pocket, pulling out a five-spot. "Here. You're on your own. Get an education, Westley." I didn't understand. "That woman with the snake standing over there in front of the tent? She or one of her con-artist friends will slip that fiver right out of your hand without you ever knowing. Make it last, boy. The night'll be sweeter. I'll meet you back here in a couple hours. I just might not recognize you."

"Why?"

"You might be turned into a man."

We met outside the carnival grounds two hours later.

"So what did you do, son?" He ground the car's accelerator.

"Oh, just wandered around."

"Did you check out the snake lady's tent?" He knew I hadn't.

Disgruntled, he inquired if I had seen my uncle among the carnies. "He was probably in one of those damn tents." Instead of heading home, he steered our old Dodge toward the center of town.

"Which uncle?"

"My brother Felix. He used to work these shows, you know?"

Pap always preached that you picked your friends. *"God gives you your relatives."* They could've all been dead as far as he was concerned.

"I heard his voice coming from one of those barkers over at a carnival in Sharon once. The ingrate hiding under a clown face, cob-nosed with huge ears, wearin' a donkey's erection and waving his arms like a windmill, coaxing all the men to go inside his tent to see the 'Niagara Falls Girl.'"

"You haven't ever told me none of this, Pap."

"You ain't ever asked." His pink-veined eyes sharply met mine.

Our car was now swerving up Mill Street. His thoughts were ricocheting. Father rolled his window down and gulped the night air. "Where'n the hell are we headed anyway, boy?" he cried.

"Pap, did you speak to Uncle Felix that night in Sharon?"

"Christ, you know your brother in any company no matter how gussied up he is. But he pretended he didn't recognize me."

"Why wouldn't he speak with you?"

"Because he abandoned his wife and kids back here in Hebron without a goddamn dime between them. That's why!"

He lay on the horn for a few seconds. Wasn't nobody around.

"Pap, I never knew any of this."

"Never a damn word. Went off and became a lion tamer. Stuck his head inside the critter's mouth, if you can believe that."

At the post office we stopped short for a red light.

"A lion tamer?"

"Uh-huh. Eva, my sister, strips for the Elks 'n' your Uncle Stephen's a monsignor in the Holy Roman Catholic Church too—if you can make any sense of that!" As if he'd let off a firecracker inside the Dodge. "Yeah, go on and say it. *'Holy shit, Pap!'*"

"Why haven't you ever told Jeremiah and me?"

He didn't answer.

"Did Uncle Felix ever go up on a trapeze?"

"If he smelled pussy he might've." We'd begun to slow down. "I'm hungry. How 'bout you, boy?" He pulled our car up in front of Coney Island, a chili dog establishment. I ordered two with everything and a buttermilk; he ordered his dogs and a bottle of Fort Pitt.

"You knew your grandfather Jake Muller built the Washington Street and Jefferson Avenue bridges right here in the center of town?"

"I knew that."

"But a mean son of a bitch, huh?" Grabbing a dog, he swung himself into the booth. "When he drank, he liked to punish Felix, stringin' him up by his thumbs on leather loops screwed in the doorway between our Jefferson Avenue flat's kitchen and living room—then whippin' the piss out of him with a cat-o'-nine-tails."

Pap slapped his calloused hand against the leatherette booth.

"Your uncle always had that beautiful western outfit on, white silk shirt with mother-of-pearl buttons, the kind that go a quarter of the way up your arm," Pap rhapsodized, "and white twill riding jodhpurs, and those shellacked black hand-tooled boots with a nosebleed-red cardinal embossed right into each of their sides . . . little mustard-seed eyes cut into their heads. Even had one tattooed onto his back shoulder."

He leaned over real close. The onions weren't masking the whiskey.

"The old man used to beat him so bad . . . come home late from the saloon every night looking for Felix. The nuns would go down to the bridge work site and snitch to the old man that Felix wasn't showing up for school.

"'Where in the hell's your brother?' he'd rage at Stephen and me. We all slept in the same bed, and Felix'd be wedged between the bed and the wall, hiding.

"'Joey, where's your sonofabitchin' brother?' I ain't ever done that to you or Jeremiah—have I?"

Pap ate his frank in three gulps.

"I came home from school once and saw Ma huddled over in the corner, crossing herself, worrying the rosary like somebody'd died. In the dark kitchen doorway was your uncle, hanging by his thumbs.

"'Ma!' I yelled. Like she didn't hear me.

"'Don't touch him,' she cautioned flatly. 'Your father put him up. Says he'll take him down.'

"'Joey . . .' Felix whispered.

"'What?'

"'Outside on the windowsill. Look.'

"I saw only the brick of the neighboring tenement an arm's length away.

"'That bird,' he said. 'The cardinal . . . see it sittin' there starin' in at me? Do ya?'

"Weren't nothing there, Westley.

"'Grab it for me, Joey. Sneak up 'n' grab it for me.' Felix hanging there—laughing. "'Don't scare it away. Grab it. I'll open my mouth real wide—you bring it to my face and I'll swallow it whole, feathers and all.'"

"'Jesus Christ . . . why would you want to do that?' I asked.

"Mother was chanting the rosary, and Felix, looking older than Jake, says, '*Because I want to swallow my heart, that's fucking why!*'"

Pap looked at me like he wanted to cry.

* * *

"To Swallow His Heart" might well be a companion piece to the "Monks" installment. The narrator is cast into an unfamiliar though captivating environment. From the father's point of view, upon exiting the carnival's gate, the son has failed the manhood test. Likewise, when the narrator quits the monastery's grounds, we can assume he's disappointed his friend, Arthur, and is not about to become a novice in the Trappist order.

Sex and celibacy. Yet he opts for neither.

What jumped out at me were the personas of Felix and Stephen viewed independent of their backstories. *It's as though the narrator is uncertain who he is.* Shorn of any real identity, he is attracted to these antithetical ones. It's not for the accompanying storylines but simply for what they represent: a priest and a clown.

And the more I pondered this, the even greater significance I attributed to "Going Dark."

I was now viewing Westley at the critical moment of being lured by these two irreconcilable identities . . . yet he felt he could not adequately perform either.

The midway and the church.

Why couldn't he embrace both?

I could now better comprehend the demented old monk and plaster saints metaphor: a multicolored flame leaping off its wick in a votive glass, unique among the plethora of fiery orange ones in the nave; the midway denizen chanting "Kyrie, eleison" while weighing one's sins for a dime.

The crux of it all was that my journey was a quest for meaning. My brother was on that very same path.

And to save ourselves, we had to reconcile.

I was both elated and diminished by this insight.

And that evening, awaiting sleep, I saw the jelly jars' green lights flickering on my ceiling like cicadas in headlights on deathly humid nights.

* * *

So if and when I found Westley, I should not be surprised at his inability to square with me, to confess that his character was an impermanent one. I feared that he was locked into these two identities, performed at separate intervals. As if channeling Felix and Stephen, our paternal uncles.

While working this through in my head, a disturbing thought suggested itself:

Was he holding firm to either of these two personas, switching from one to another, to engage, in an all-encompassing and conflicting manner, the identities in stark contrast to each other so as to keep his mind from returning to the bridge?

The roles his life preservers, so to speak?

In one he performed the role of God's shepherd, whereas on the midway or under a tent he cast himself as an entertainer, proficient in make-believe or dupery. Besides, the multifarious pageantry of each persona helped him become larger than life enables us to be.

And I thought back to "The Window Harp," where the two brothers, often left alone, occupied themselves for hours on end scripting and performing Punch and Judy–like dramas.

Had Westley gone back to his childhood to seek refuge?

And why did this all seem so familiar to me?

CHAPTER TEN

FIND HIM BY BECOMING HIM

What was the evidence that I was on the cusp of meeting my brother?

Yes, I knew more about him than when I began. It's also true I sometimes felt we were virtually one. That I was, in fact, Jeremiah, and soon the three of us would be united, with Westley commending me for having so rigorously pursued the quest when often even he might have given up.

But truthfully, I was no closer to connecting with him than I had been when we were absolute strangers.

It was all in my head.

I'd believed I would encounter geographical evidence in his stories that I could trace. Failing in that effort, I chased the seminary lead, following his various pastoral assignments with what I perceived to be some success. Except I was no closer to physically meeting him than would be a biographer of his long deceased subject.

In truth, I had been fooling myself.

Did I require more evidence that the acid-green lights on the bridge had illuminated the pathway to this bilious-tasting self-awareness?

And that evening—concluding that even the initial visit to my father to bid him good-bye had been, at best, a naive one—I was still acting out the child, deceiving myself that it was the honorable gesture a son owed his father.

"Made in God's image" had imploded, fallen in upon itself. I was nothing. Nobody. A ready-made self handed to me at birth that I had willed myself to grow into. Then one day it will breathe its final breath in me and I will deflate.

I lay in bed watching the car lights outside my window circle on my ceiling and thought about feeling my way, hand over hand, on the bridge's parapet to its center. There would be no phoning my father this time. Enough of that. Let them recall me as they created me. Who was I anyway? My brother's keeper?

And that brought a caustic grin to my face.

How about if this is where we reunite, I thought. *At its center. One of us has to go first. Am I braver than you?*

And then I recalled his story. But was it mine? I no longer knew for certain. For I had been at this very place before. I distinctly recall my father saying, "Hold on."

"This is an emergency, lady. My number is 7-6208, Sharon exchange. Charge it to me." I could hear him mutter, "My boy's in some kind of distress." She kept repeating, *Five cents, please, deposit another five cents.* "Christ, can't you hear me, lady? Santa Muerte, festooned with green lights, is winging my kid across the dark Allegheny—and they're about to merge with the fucking Ohio! It'll be in all the papers in the morning if you don't let us continue this conversation."

Then nothing.

All we could hear was each other taking air. And for what seemed a whole minute, surely a dime's worth, we breathed heavy, sucked wind, scrambling away from Mr. Taps.

Cajoling the operator not to cut us off.

For his boy was about to find his way to Huck and Jim's proverbial raft.

It could be Westley's and mine. Maybe that's where we would converge: down at the mouth of the Mississippi. And start all over, this time creating ourselves, christening ourselves with our own names, abandoning the pasts that were never truly ours anyway.

And if fortune smiled upon us, one identity would suffice for navigating the rapids surely ahead of us.

It was at this moment that I sat up, faced my bedroom window, and saw him staring back at me.

"Westley," I murmured, fearing I would cause him to vanish. But he continued to stare at me, unblinking.

"What is it?" I asked. "Please answer me."

I slowly crawled out of bed and stepped to the window. He had not moved. As I got closer, I urged him to speak. "Call my name. Something. Identify yourself, for Christ's sake and your unholy brother's."

I moved my face to the window and pleaded with him not to move his. Then, as if from some long-buried memory, I placed my lips to his and sang a lament. And the pane buzzed.

The window harp sang in my room that night.

I wept to his image.

As he surely did to mine, for the room wept in a harp's despairing tone. A keening of sorts, an unholy song of separation. A longing for the selves to be reunited.

He warbling to me, I to him.

And somewhere in this hymn of lost brothers, I begged for him not to leave. And if he would stay . . . so would I.

For I could foresee in his eyes that dark night what he wished to say to me if he could have spoken.

But he couldn't, for it was my voice, my tongue, my utterance.

He could only signal by his eyes that at the most intense moment of that brief encounter, they appeared as headlights on our family car, and I saw them stopping before me as I climbed the parapet, blinking on and off, as if in fright that I could go through with it.

The headlights nearly blinded me, letting me know I wasn't alone. There was somebody inside that automobile, signaling me to stop.

And I did.

I did, understanding that if I left, he had no choice but to leave also.

An epiphany on the bridge of acid-green lights.

When daylight broke, I knew what I must do. It couldn't have been more evident. I would join him in the very same way he'd joined other identities in "Going Dark." I would become my brother as a means to reunite us.

This was the true pathway to discovering him.

His appearance in the window told me that.

I would become Westley Mueller.

BOOK TWO

PART ONE

THE METAMORPHOSIS

CHAPTER ONE

It is as if [Genet] recognized that during the brief period when he acted as a normal representative of French society, he was as absurd as that society itself—doubly so, since he was only impersonating a normal man.[2]

His photograph in tennis whites at the seminary would be my starting point. The manuscripts, my primer. Amused that he was more real to me than my anodyne self, how could I not effect verisimilitude? Who was the chrysalis unveiled?

As we sat across from each other at the Gorge, I recalled Papa's admonition regarding Westley's writings: *Having read much of what's in here . . . I believe it may have been written with you in mind. He surely suspected your mother was with child prior to his departure. He awaits you, Ethan.*

But it will not be revealed to you easily.

And as the moments passed, I began to sense that this person I'd never touched had sat alongside me, offering an encouraging *yes* when I began telling his story, now mine. Scribbling away, I experienced a palpable sense of abandonment. We were conspirators of sorts. At times, it felt as if he had begun placing the words onto my tablet. As if to say: *Here, let me do it.*

At one point, I thought I'd heard someone at my door and, when I found no one there and returned to my chair, a stranger in a man's felt hat stood grinning back at me in a wall mirror. "West-ley?" I asked.

"Hurry back to your chair," he said. "Oh, Christ yes, write."

It was as if I had begun giving birth to myself; for now, as the hours elapsed, one sentence after another took form with an au-thority foreign to me. No equivocation. And each time I passed that mirror as late afternoon succumbed to evening, the hatted gentleman was no longer a stranger.

He was the Normal Man.

Why I Wrote Those Stories

I'd always wanted to be a Normal Man, one who wore a wide-brimmed hat, a fine suit, and shoes that took a burnished shine and lasted for several years. I wanted to own a recent-model automobile with a bespoke wife in the passenger seat, a child or two in the backseat, a brick house hedged by rose bushes, and a backyard where we'd gather with friends on a summer evening.

Normal men did not reside in our neighborhood.

I'd stroll down elm-canopied streets on their north side of town, where manicured lawns ran long distances from grand homes. Gazing into their rooms, I'd imagine one ensconced in a leather chair while awaiting dinner, the interior lit as if by dying embers; the plump beds on the second floor dressed in cloud-white sheets and pillowcases; and the tiled, clotted-cream bathrooms with nickel fixtures and beveled mirrors.

There were, of course, mirrors in our house. I'd feign being the son of a Normal Man by daubing my hair with a fragrant pomade and combing it with a distinct part while standing before a mirror next to my father, who'd sprinkle blue cologne on his chest in preparation for going out for the evening. Except he knew who stared back at him. As did the scarlet women he'd rendezvous with later.

Mother, who loathed the looking glass, suffered bouts of depression and had an ongoing liaison with death. Escaping into the arms of Christ occupied her waking hours, whereas Papa didn't believe in postponing rapture for what he couldn't touch.

I had friends who thought the Normal Man lived on the other side of town, too. Except they never hoped to become one. "How can you become somebody you aren't?" they'd ask.

But I aspired to a life where days weren't defined by dystopian surprises. Though I was enamored of them in my dreams, I was not inspired by my father's dalliances, his absorption in louche women. And as for my dear but troubled mother, she, too, would happily have led me up a blind alley.

Inept at sports, I had become immune to the shame of being the last one chosen when sides were picked. Ironically, it was my acting the part of the scion of a Normal Man that caused others to take a benign and risible liking to me: I attended church regularly, never cussed, answered *Yes ma'am* and *No sir* when addressing adults, treated the opposite sex deferentially, and excused myself when they shadowed Rosa Nowiki into the woods. Since I trusted that I was created in God's image, it was not in my interest to leave any stains. Occasionally in the schoolyard after dark, I'd be cajoled to list all the possible sins that I'd never commit. It was as if I were reciting the stats of Ralph Kiner or Roberto Clemente. I laughed along with my friends.

I was the ersatz Normal Man's son.

My friend Anthony's father had one leg and owned the one-pump gas station at the bottom of our street. He spent his working days mostly in the grease pit under the canopies of aged cars. Larry's father was a Pentecostal preacher who sold Electrolux vacuum cleaners door to door. Ben's "old man" was retired and morbidly obese, and could only steer his aged Buick; Ben would be summoned to shift the gears on their way for groceries.

One sunny day while school was in recess, Larry asked me to recite the Twenty-Third Psalm for his father. The man wore a brush mustache and had his hair parted down the middle. His mouth formed a tight oval when speaking as if he were miming one of the vacuum's accessories. The part-time cleric nodded approvingly and cast a chiding look at his son. He invited me to his church the following Sunday, but Mother nixed my attending because "those folks speak in tongues."

Her barely disguised scorn confused me because when unduly depressed, she'd stand against the hallway window at some point during the night and, placing her lips against the pane, would begin to mewl, creating an unnerving glass harmonium.

Over time it began to dawn on me that in order to survive, I had to become somebody other than who I was.

And, if I was created in the image of God, who was that?

It's why, after considerable bedevilment, I chose the Normal Man for my role model. Who but he, I surmised, would earnestly aspire to fulfill the promise of his maker's image?

Soon I began comporting myself as his presumed son. I worked after school and on Saturdays for a florist whose clientele resided on the north side. Delivering floral arrangements, I became accustomed to entering hushed Georgian interiors with hardwood foyers; some were brightly papered and well lit, while others were less welcoming. Ample dining rooms were furnished with the requisite Chippendale furniture to accommodate several guests, and the living rooms were graced with an abundance of overstuffed chairs, often Queen Annes, of course, and sofas in muted fabrics. Oriental carpets were *de rigueur.*

It was generally the Normal Man's wife who would call out when I rang the bell to place the vase of, say, tulips or irises on the breakfront or on the grand piano in the living room. Since we delivered flowers for births, weddings, and funerals, and even decorated the burial plots in the cemetery—a glade of white birches and towering elms traversed by pebble pathways—I became intimately accustomed to the lives of many of the Hill customers through my early high school years.

It wasn't long before I began to express a liking for a number of the Normal Men's daughters, a natural outgrowth of my believing that I belonged. For one classmate, to whom I was especially attracted, I'd filch a dozen of red roses or fashion an orchid corsage at the florist shop and then on a general delivery drop the "secret admirer" box off at her house, always feigning ignorance as to the sender.

If I kept the secret, nobody, especially me, would get hurt.

The role was growing on me, and over time I realized, paradoxically, that I was better off *playing* the role of a Normal Man's son than being one. *I was not captive to the identity as if I had been granted it at birth.* I relished the notion that I was creating my own persona by adopting the traits and characteristics of having been born on the other side of town . . . while knowing full well that, in truth, I was nobody.

It all began to make profound sense to me—having been created in God's image.

* * *

But, about to embark on my last year in high school, I had begun to tire of impersonation. Despite being practiced in the ways of the Normal Man, knowing in my heart that I was still a nonentity was quite honestly more gratifying to me than the diminishing returns coming from my role.

It felt as if the entire "God's image" mien was crumbling.

I began writing my thoughts down and found relief of a sort unique to me. It was equal to and often greater than the satisfaction that resulted when the onlookers truly believed I was the person I feigned being.

And a month into my senior year, I found myself withdrawing even more. Friends queried what was going on. I'd answer that it had nothing to do with them, that there were troubles at home. But the truth was that earlier on, a large part of who I was had depended on their accepting me. This was no longer the case.

I had someone else who fulfilled that need now. He was five years younger, and I wrote about him almost every day.

And for the first time in memory, I was truly somebody . . . *Jeremiah's brother.*

CHAPTER TWO

JEREMIAH'S BROTHER

He was becoming as real to me as I was to myself. We laughed often in the dark confines of my bedroom, and his presence mitigated the anguish I experienced when Momma went to the hallway window. I'd awaken him when Papa returned home long after midnight upon hearing her pad down the stairs.

I no longer aspired to be the grown son of the Normal Man, having come to judge that act as an empty existence. Not unlike, in truth, what I was now living. But at least I knew it and could no longer keep up the appearance.

Then one day I begin chronicling the life of this mystery brother. What endeared him to me most was his irreverence, a veritable tonic for me. It no longer mattered that much to me what was occurring outside our bedroom door. We had each other. And those times when I felt dispirited, Jeremiah would perform a little dance on our bed.

Christ, I often thought, *where have you been?*

There were moments when I'd wonder why he had showed up at this point in my life. Everything about him was authentic, the total opposite of me, really. He joked about my prudishness; my inability to swear; the Sunday School homilies I'd recite; my fear of eternal damnation; and above all my admonishing him, when he blasphemed, that each of us was created in God's image.

His usual retort to that chastisement: "Not me, brother. It's why I'm so goddamned lucky."

Those words darkly presaged what was soon to occur to me. I couldn't have known it then, but in looking back upon that time, it seems clear that was why Jeremiah entered my life.

I've lifted from my journals an excerpt detailing the incident:

* * *

THE VISITOR
(excerpt)

If I acceded to its logic, surely the voice would stop badgering me. One spring morning, I suggested, "If I agree to a time and place for the act, will you promise to leave me alone for a while?"

The voice hesitated.

I persisted. "I'll give you the name of the time and place when I will perform the act if you permit me to enjoy my last days in relative peace. It's a fair request, is it not?"

Name it, then.

"Promise?"

Name it, and I'll lay off. However, if you fail to carry out your end of our bargain, Westley . . . I will have no mercy.

"Washington Street bridge, second Sunday morning in April—at daybreak. One condition: if the sun doesn't appear, we postpone it to the following Sunday."

It laughed, another first. But always, I'd done what I promised.

The following morning I crossed the bridge. In the past the voice would have compelled me to the parapet's edge to peer far down at the cascading water, inquiring, *Can you see yourself floating down toward the south side of Hebron, Westley? There you are! See the blissful grin on your face? For Christ's sake, do it. Now!*

I did see my face, but I saw others, too. Those of the male residents in the City Rescue Mission abutting the Neshannock on the south side of the bridge. Reflections of pale faces smashed up against the windows of the Mission's spartan rooms. The morning sun ignited both its glass and surface of the water. Among their faces was mine. Did they periodically jump too? I wondered. Perhaps at night, guiding their way down into the black Neshannock by moonlight?

Three-quarters of the way across the bridge, I still hadn't been accosted. The bridge had lost its curse, and for the first time in several months, I could answer *Here* for morning attendance and not be lying.

* * *

That afternoon, I called Jeremiah up to our room.

"I haven't been able to talk to you or anybody else what's been happening to me, Jeremiah. But I'm OK now." And embraced him.

He squirmed. "It's no fun not having you around. Are you lovesick?"

I laughed. "Jesus . . . yes, maybe I was. I thought I was gonna die." We lay in our bed, coiled, rocking back and forth and giddily laughing for reasons neither of us fully understood.

That evening, we walked towards the Neshannock River at the edge of town.

"Why'd you want to meet me, Westley?"

"I lied to you this morning. I was lovesick—but no woman was involved."

Jeremiah instinctively drew back.

"It isn't that, either."

The streetlights were farther apart now.

"Weeks ago, one Monday morning when I awoke, well, there were two of us—*me* and another *me*. I could barely get dressed for school that morning, the bickering inside my head got so deafening. 'Maybe it will go away,' I think. You know sometimes how you get double vision?"

He began walking ahead of me.

"Two voices arguing with each other!" I said.

"Like you and me?" he asked.

"Just like it. I go upstairs, pick out my favorite shirt to wear. All the time, this other voice is mocking how fucking stupid it looks. *What the hell are you even dressing for, going to school?* 'Shut the fuck up!' I reply. Jeremiah, I holler at you to shut up, huh? But to scream at myself to shut the fuck up? And in the mirror?"

Jeremiah looked like Pap in the dark. Same build, a shadow over his face like the one the old man's downturned fedora cast, and like his mind was off somewhere. "You gonna be all right, Westley?"

"So listen . . . this son of a bitch pops the question on me."

"Who, Westley! Who in Christ's name we talking about!"

"I don't know who!"

"What'd he say?"

"'*You're a no-good fucking simple bastard, Westleymueller.*'"

Jeremiah started to laugh.

"'*Life makes no goddamn sense,*' it bellowed. '*Give me one simple reason why you should go on living, Westleymueller.*' The prick's so much brighter than I am, brother."

Jeremiah palmed a Zippo lighter and thumbed its wheel against the flint, and the flame illuminated his hazel eyes, just like the old man's. But his registered alarm. "Smoke?"

"Listen. The fucker says it's all a joke. Even you. Says you're doomed just like me. And I'm a prick coward 'cause I know it . . ."

His shoe ground the cigarette into the gravel.

"I ask you, do you get it?"

"Yeah, yeah . . . I get it," he said.

We headed back toward the eatery in town.

"Westley?"

"Yeah."

"Whatta you gonna do?"

"We got a date."

"Who?"

"The voice 'n' me."

Jeremiah stopped walking.

"We're to meet on the bridge one Sunday morning at daybreak. Then I'll know."

"Know what?"

"That the water's bitter cold . . . or I'm no longer a ninety-pound weakling."

But he wasn't responding to my forced attempt at downplaying what I'd revealed, for it had clearly upset him.

"Look, you and I are going to get out of here, Jeremiah." I put my arm around him.

"You promise?"

"Yeah . . . and you know why?"

"Why?"

"'Cause ain't none of this shit for real!" I spun around, gesturing to the town. "It's all man-made, every last goddamn bit of it except the moon, the stars, and the fucking grass. You 'n' me, Jeremiah, we ain't doomed like your calvary man across there—look at the poor bastard. The stores across the street—look inside them, too, brother. Mannequins standing around, all dressed up like dandies. And the Episcopal church across the Diamond—clink your offering in its silver trays. For what? Up on the North Hill inside our big red schoolhouse, what do they bore us with every day? *Illusions*, Jeremiah!

"Who ever said any of it was for real?"

* * *

I didn't cross the Washington Street Bridge after work. By the time I arrived home, there was only a light on in the basement. Mother was in the cellar ironing our shirts. Jeremiah and Father had gone out. I wrapped my week's pay and the remainder of my savings in an elastic and stuffed the bills into the toe of one of Father's wingtips in his closet. When he found it, he'd be in the money. I walked down and kissed her good night. My softball mitt, and darkroom chemicals, trays, and photographic paper, all lying on the workbench behind her. *They belong to Jeremiah now*, I thought.

"Westley," she called up to me at the landing. "Is everything OK?"

"Why?"

"Saturday night? Home this early and going to bed?"

"We were busy at the florist shop today. I'm fine, Ma. See you in the morning."

I studied the United States presidents on our wallpaper, the large and small fissures in the plaster ceiling to which I'd given mythical river names. A bookcase containing the set of *Encyclopedia Americana* that a crony had sold to my father in a saloon one Saturday afternoon sat in the corner like an unused parlor piano.

For years he bragged to anybody who would listen that Jeremiah and I could look up anything we ever wanted to know. That all the mysteries of the universe sat at the bottom of our bed.

Waiting.

* * *

Before daybreak, while the others were still asleep, I crept out of the house. Washington Street looked like a tired movie set awaiting a new script—not a car or a pedestrian in sight. The houses of worship wouldn't sound their summoning bells until 9:00 a.m. Workers had recently blasted rust off the bridge's steel members, then primed these spots bright orange. The lesions contrasted garishly with its weathered coats of aluminum and chalked graffiti.

Entering the trestle, I felt I was negotiating a skeletal, industrial-age vault. Muffled pigeon cooing merged with the sounds of the river rushing against the span's supports. The chromium daylight illuminated a canister of lilies with powdery mustard-colored stamens I'd placed in the Lutz Florist window the night before. Large river rats nested in the shop's cutting shaft, a steamy warmth luring them deeper inside the fermenting womb.

I waited for a signal.

Where in Christ's name was he?

Man and boy mannequins in Summers Haberdashery's foyer, attired in wide-brimmed fedoras and pistachio-green suits, mocked my apprehension, while Sydney Pearlman, who wore bright fuchsia stockings, scurried to his store.

Downstream, ochre smokestacks towered above cavernous mill buildings. The nascent sun ignited the refinery's casement windows etched with decades of a rust bath. These shafts of light hung like diaphanous scrims from the steel rafters at contrasting planes, then periodically shimmered, flying up, as if they were the garments of an unseen Hephaestus.

Was I alone? Was he not going to show?

No young men this day waiting to dive for coins tossed by the bridge passersby, and I bent over the parapet as far as I could without tumbling headlong... Only darkness and washing noises there.

"HELLO!"

My call reverberated under the bridge to oblivion, "*Oh, oh, oh, oh.*"

Had I called his bluff?

"HELLO!" Again the dark gallery under this massive iron cranium with orange spots on its bones answered, "*Oh, oh, oh, oh.*"

Finally, I turned to leave the bridge, when . . .

Damn close, prick. I never miss an appointment.

"Perhaps you've got too many," I said.

Let's cut the shit and get it over with.

"I have one question."

Yes?

"Your name?"

The pigeons burst skyward, creating a deafening ruckus up inside the cranial arches of the bridge.

You don't know?

"No."

Westley, it said.

"Westley?"

Yes. Westley Mueller.

"But wait . . ."

I thought you'd figured it out.

"There can't be two of us," I said.

There won't be, it replied.

It was then I visualized Jeremiah, shaking his head at me from across the bridge and mouthing "no."

I turned.

Where are you going?

"Home."

Oh no, you made a promise.

"You got it," I replied.

I crossed the street in front of Hebron Dry Goods.

What do you mean, 'You got it'?

"Westleymueller!" I began laughing, running up alongside the Ne-shannock.

Hey, you fucker! Come back here. Coward!

"What'd you say your name is?" I cried.

Westley Mueller, he replied unapologetically.

"That's what I thought you said. YOU'RE THE PRICK COWARD, Westley!"

I ran back to the bridge and stood at its center. The fire-orange sun had bled out of the water below. It looked icy blue, with a pale saffron light washing the storied brick and multiwindowed City Rescue Mission.

"Jump, you motherfucker, or are you the coward?" I cried.

No answer.

"I don't hear you moving. Cat got your tongue?"

The pigeons exploded out of their nests, swooping through the grids on toward town. Only the water below chortled.

"WHERE ARE YOU, WESTLEY MUELLER?"

No. You are Westley. I am not Westley.

"Then who are you?"

It answered again: *I am not Westley.* But its voice kept getting weaker, as if it'd begun to walk away from me.

"Wait!" I cried.

I am not Westley. I am not Westley.

"If you are not Westley, then who? Let's settle this once and for all."

The voice no longer answered.

In Pearlman's window, Sydney Pearlman stood in fuchsia stocking feet, arranging gladioli in the body of the Maytag washer. As I passed, he pressed his bulbous, milky-red lips against the plate-glass window, mouthing "Westley. Westley." Overhead in the *Chronicle*'s vestibule, the pigeons cooed gutturally inside a medieval brass lantern.

"Where are you, Westley?" I cried once more.

Crossing the street, I walked briskly back toward the bridge, pretending I no longer saw Sydney. Inside Lutz's doorway—a black Chinese lacquered showcase with burnished frond-shaped hardware. Orchids and cymbidiums rising out of narrow-necked goblets glowed eerily in its fluorescent light.

Did the voice wish to speak once again?

Inside the bridge, I cried out, "Well, are you in here, coward?"

But newly washed automobiles rolled under the girders, heading toward the houses of worship. I glanced over the parapet. The river now calm, lucent. The midmorning sun cast shafts of radiant light down through the Washington Street Bridge's riveted frame. Soon it and the primer-orange spots would be painted a bright aluminum—in time for Easter, perhaps.

Back up the hill alongside the Neshannock, several times I summoned Westley without a response. *The name didn't fit you any better than it did me,* I reasoned, laughing at the top of my lungs while sprinting home as rapidly as a man's legs could carry him.

* * *

Recalling that period, I had to acknowledge that despite my braggadocio, I alone hadn't outfoxed the voice terrorizing me. Jeremiah and I had. It was his presence on the bridge that morning that saved me. *He was someone to live for.*

CHAPTER THREE

A NORMAL MAN'S DAUGHTER

As time passed, I cryptically imagined us as the Chang and Eng brothers of our town, the most famous of the conjoined twins. And I fantasized that he and I, like that pair, lived together for the remainder of our lives alongside our wives and many children.

I could never let him know that, of course. And even when he began spending more time away from the house, I understood his need to break away from passing all our free time together. Also, he revered Papa for making a life for himself.

"Why should he be prisoner to Momma's demons?" he'd ask.

He'd borrow Papa's shoes when he dressed up to go out.

I can't say that I was at all surprised when one night he confided that he had a crush on a classmate of his, the only daughter of the most prominent undertaker in our town, who lived in a fine estate in the community where the Normal Men resided. And it wasn't long before he announced the mortician had taken "a shine" to him, offering him a Saturday job washing all the funeral cars at Slade Hyde.

Since I had delivered floral arrangements to Hebron's mortuaries, I was quite familiar with that one. Service people had to enter through the rear, past the hearse, flower car, and limousines. The shade of Slade Hyde's 1930s Chrysler and Packard fleet was deep indigo. Set off from them was an exquisite hearse with elaborate carved mahogany paneling around and under the oblong windows of its viewing compartment.

"That's the one I want," Jeremiah exclaimed, referring to the Packard Phaeton V12 hearse. "Christ, she's a beauty."

But it was his unmitigated bravado that unsettled me. He honestly believed that it was just a matter of time before he would be residing in that grand residence and have access to all those antique automobiles, plus one of the loveliest young women in town.

Long after he'd fallen asleep, I'd lie awake, worrying about his fate.

* * *

JEREMIAH FALLS FOR A NORMAL MAN'S DAUGHTER

Jeremiah had acquired a penchant for exploring the unknown. Scaring the shit out of people, throwing himself into the teeth of danger, and then, after the show, when everybody went home—he'd crawl back out.

When he told me he was seeing Judith Hyde, I wasn't surprised. Judith's father owned the most prominent mortuary in town, and that summer it wasn't uncommon to hear her pull up in our driveway in her indigo-blue convertible, looking for Jeremiah. I'd go out to speak with her when he was sleeping or not around. I complained to him about it, saying he should be more considerate.

He thought it was funny. "Who are you afraid of, Westley?"

"Nobody."

"You got to learn how to treat a woman."

"From you?"

"You can't be afraid of them."

"I'm not afraid of women."

"The real ones, you are," he said. "The kind that chew your balls off, huh? Not Jeremiah Mueller. I grab their headlights and yank them right to me. Laugh in their faces. That's when they bend. That's how to treat Mr. Taps, too."

"What are you talking about?"

"Remember when you found Mama bent over the canning stove in the cellar? Mr. Taps smells like a woman."

"You're full of shit, Jeremiah."

"Do you think men hang themselves 'cause they want to die?"

His impish grin curled up, revealing a splinter of teeth. "Huh-uh. They do it because they smell cunt."

"You saying death smells like a woman?"

"Under the armpits. Between the legs."

"You got a big imagination, too."

"Mr. Taps smells just like a broad." Jeremiah's face was one of intense resolve.

"Sure," I said, half mocking.

* * *

Judith phoned after nine o'clock that Saturday evening. "Has he left the house yet?" "Tell her I'm leaving now," Jeremiah answered, and rolled back to sleep. She called at nine thirty, then ten. "Westley, lie for Chrissake!" He jumped up both times, switched off the overhead light, and fell back into our bed.

"Jeremiah's sleeping, isn't he, Westley?" It was after eleven.

I didn't answer.

"Well, you don't have to protect him any longer. Tell him not to bother showing up."

Minutes later he came down the stairs, fully dressed to go out.

"She's pissed, Jeremiah."

"They bore you to tears when they aren't," he said.

It was Mrs. Hyde who phoned at 2:00 a.m. Pap wasn't home. Mother hollered up the stairs, "Jeremiah's in some kind of trouble, Westley." Mother handed me the phone. Judith was on the line.

Jeremiah had taken her out the Old Wilmington Road for a ride. She was angry because of his apathy. "Always late, Westley," as she put it. "I'm tired of it. Sometimes even missing our date."

"Where is he?" I asked.

"You know the ravine behind Cringle's farm? Down in there somewhere."

"What do you mean?"

"He got hot over something I said. Stepped on the accelerator, began double- and triple-shifting—taking the country roads at high speed. I wanted out, but he kept accusing me."

"Of what?"

"What else? What causes you men to go nuts?"

"Who is it, Judith?"

"Your brother asked me what I was doing Sunday evening. 'You and I aren't doing anything,' I tell him. 'I've got a date.' That's when he throttled it."

"Is he hurt?"

"I don't know. We're heading straight down Cliff Road when he stiffens and jams on the brakes. The car fishtails. He opens his door and Johnny Weissmullers into the gorge."

"Not a drop of water runs through that canyon, Judith. Did you go looking for him?"

I heard the whoosh of her cigarette lighter.

"You considered that he might be lying down in that ravine *dead*?"

"Jeremiah Mueller, *dead*?" She laughed. "Fat chance—and when he does come up out of that ravine, tell him Mama and me decided I won't be seeing him again. He's not to phone me up either."

* * *

We didn't know much about psychiatrists then. Only mental institutions like neighboring Dixmont employed them. Jeremiah began staying up in our room and refused to come downstairs.

"You sure I can't fix you something to eat?" Mother asked.

He wanted nothing to do with me either, but lay up in the bedroom plotting—we weren't certain what. Pap sat on the side of the bed to speak with him.

"How you feeling, son?"

"Did she call?" Jeremiah asked.

When no one answered, he never looked up.

Then Judith's mother phoned again because Jeremiah had shown up, parking himself on their porch.

Mother twisted a paper napkin over in her fingers. "Oh, Mrs. Hyde," Mother sighed.

Jeremiah had pressed his face right up against their screen door until Judith yelled, "Get off the damn porch!" and slammed the door.

"Not my nature to be sharing a woman . . . but I apologize," Jeremiah said, and walked down off the steps, opened his car door, waved . . . then pulled his necktie taut behind his neck and jerked his head out of his collar like he was hanging himself.

"All the neighbors watching, Mrs. Mueller, and he just kept bawling out her name."

I could only wait for what I knew was soon to occur. Mother, Papa, and I knew he was planning on his next dramatic move. We feared that it might be his final act.

The worrying over Jeremiah's mental well-being had become a catalyst for bringing our parents together in a way I'd never experienced. Papa began hanging around the house after work. It was not unusual to see the two of them sitting quietly in the living room together, or on the front porch swing conversing.

Mother had ceased padding to the hallway window after dark to play the glass harmonium.

* * *

THIS SIDE OF THE MAGNOLIA TREES

"Jesus stands outside our bedroom door," Jeremiah said.

When the lights in the house were extinguished and everybody was in bed, he'd crawl out of ours and place his ear to the door.

"What are you listening for?" I asked

"The circus man."

"The circus man?"

"They pounded nails into his hands and feet, didn't they? He's some courageous dude. I want to hear his breathing."

There were nights we heard nothing. Then we did.

"Come here, Westley," he whispered. "Hurry!"

I slipped out of bed and put my head beside his against our wooden door. Heavy breathing. Then a kind of low moaning.

"Christ," he whispered. "He's reliving the event. They're pounding him to the cross. Oh, can't you just see it?"

Then we heard, "*Yes . . . sweet Jesus, yes.*"

"But it sounds like Mama," I protested.

That's when Jeremiah slapped me hard against my backside and began rolling over on the linoleum floor in laughter.

"You gullible queer!" he cried.

He jumped up onto the bed, clutching his groin.

"I'm the Circus Man!"

* * *

In a way, Jeremiah was. He never rode elephants or went up on the trapeze. But he liked to play with fire.

When I took communion for the first time—I had to learn the Twenty-third Psalm—Mother and I sat in the car, waiting for my brother to finish dressing. She was drumming on the horn to get him moving. When she heard the back door slam, she shoved her foot onto the ignition and throttled our old Dodge alive, never paying him any mind.

He looked fine, dressed in his Sunday best, but then there were these several-sizes-too-large two-tone black-and-white dancing shoes Father donned on summer evenings when he went out alone. Jeremiah had stuffed newspapers into the toe boxes and wore a solemn expression.

Anxious about whether I'd remember the Psalm, Mother handed off the bouquet of lilacs she'd freshly cut to present to me at the close of the communion.

"Jeremiah, go hand these flowers to your good brother."

When he stepped into the aisle, parishioners cupped their hands over their mouths.

"Here, queer," he announced, stumbling up the pulpit steps. "Compliments of the Circus Man."

"What's it feel like?" I asked as I lay next to him that night, feeling the heat coming off his red backside and knowing he was hurting.

"Circus men don't cry," he sniffed. "This ain't nothin'."

We knew it wasn't—for each of us could feel it in our bones that one day we'd hear *real breathing* outside our door.

* * *

Father's irreverence was more subtle.

Draping his tie over the crucifix that hung above their nuptial bed, for instance.

Or secreting spare bills he was saving for a rainy day between the pages of the Book of Revelations.

One reason for his apostasy was that our Uncle Alexander, his brother, was a monsignor. *It'd be like Jeremiah wearing the clown shoes*, I thought.

"Westley, suppose you saw your brother dressed up in a chasuble with a big silver crucifix dangling from his neck and blowing incense out of a lantern over the parishioners' heads?"

"I'd think he was in the carnival," I said.

"Not your grandmother. She believes he's her ticket to heaven. 'He's going to save us all . . . even if the rest of you heathens don't deserve it!' she'd scold. But Alexander was a snotty-nosed prick. And now he's even a bigger one in the Roman Catholic Church. But don't let me stain your mind, son. Maybe your mama is right."

I'd seen no sign that she was. Except my conscience talked like she was its ventriloquist.

* * *

Until the day Jeremiah set farmer Eli McKinley's alfalfa field on fire. Racing through it—flames curling off him like ribbon. A charred scar in his wake. And a woman in a nearby farmhouse screaming on her porch, fanning the wind, deranged.

Father's car down by the roadside, smoke puffing from under the hood. An air filter lying on the gravel alongside Jeremiah's lit cigarette— and a container of gasoline.

That's when I thought the Circus Man had finally come.

Pay up, Jeremiah. Show's over.

For months Mother, Pap, and I sat next to his hospital bed, listening to his labored breathing, his legs and arms suspended from some trapeze-like contraptions, and us barely able to see through the bandage mask he wore. Except his eyes still kindled.

I was grateful for that.

Because I was a pansy. Not a queer—but a pansy. I ached to be fearless like Jeremiah but was afraid of heaven, the scolds who professed they were happy because they were Chosen, but I knew they could never be lighthearted like Jeremiah and our old man.

Theirs was a brittle kind of rapture. If you'd promise me God wouldn't seek to avenge the irreverence, I thought the joke was on them.

* * *

Except the fire queered Jeremiah.

He wasn't entertaining any longer. Our old man began going to bed when Mother read the Bible. He no longer smoked in bed.

Jeremiah even said it was time to be moving on.

"Whaddya mean?" I asked.

"Gettin' out of here."

"What about me?" I hollered.

He rolled over without answering. The next morning I awoke to find his side of the bed empty.

The only person who didn't act surprised was Father.

"Where do you think he went?" I asked.

Jeremiah never let on. Even to him whom I know he revered. "Papa taught us to heavy breathe," he said.

At night I'd call out, "Is that you, Circus Man? Will you give me a sign?"

But it was still as sin outside our bedroom door. Only the silver light of the moon puddled on the hallway floor.

A prelude, dear brother, to your journey across a meadow just this side of the magnolia trees, just this side of hell.

CHAPTER FOUR

JEREMIAH DIED FOR ME

"Faith is believing what you know ain't so."

Jeremiah would often repeat Mark Twain's words to me. I'd laugh, brushing him off. But what perplexed me was this childlike faith that I continued to hold sacred. For there is no other word to describe its grip on me. In truth, I believed that it was such an intrinsic part of who I was, to forsake it would have been tantamount to drawing a final breath.

Why?

I was terrified of living alone, and by that I mean having only one self. There had to be someone wiser residing within me to whom I could turn in a time of need.

Even his running across that wheat field while on fire caused me to see him as larger than life, someone out of mythology, perhaps. As if he had broken through the skein of reality during that flight across the farmer's acreage.

It's the monotony of the expected that diminishes me.

All of this came rushing back to me once Jeremiah left.

PART TWO

CHAPTER FIVE

HALL OF MIRRORS

In *The Thief's Journal*, Jean Genet describes witnessing a friend trapped in a fairground's hall of mirrors. The labyrinth assemblage of transparent panes of glass and mirrors permit those assembled outside to poke fun at the victim, who curses their mockery but is helpless to escape the distorted mirror images staring back at him.

In similar respects I, too, felt as if I were trapped among various reflections of myself, none of them satisfyingly depicting who I thought I was or wished to be, but unable to escape any one of them. I often sensed that those around me were addressing one of these distorted images when socializing with me. *"Who do they see today?"* I felt an urge to cry out. *"Speak to* me, *please, the one trapped inside* here . . . *the authentic me, Westley Mueller."*

It was as if by will to become fully aware of myself, I'd been ambushed by my many selves.

* * *

As days passed, I fantasized that I was caged in that labyrinth of mirrors and windows, being paraded through the streets for the townspeople's delight. When sleep arrived, my dreams continued the script; I was the labyrinth's sole occupant, but there were several of me abandoning hope of being set free.

During this period I read omnivorously, hoping to glean a deeper self-awareness. And just as the Jean Genet description of spotting an acquaintance caught in the fairground's hall of mirrors labyrinth affected me, I was equally struck upon reading a passage in Paul Bowles's novel *The Sheltering Sky*:

Now she did not remember their many conversations built around the idea of death, perhaps because no idea about death has anything in common with the presence of death.[3]

What if I substituted God for death in the passage?

Because no idea about God has anything in common with the presence of God.

What, in truth, does any one of us know about the presence of the Supreme Being in the same way that we have experienced the presence of death? I mused.

What saint has not embraced the conviction that the human condition is, by its very nature, sinful, or pledged a lifetime of expunging all pride before the All-Merciful?

Yet is not one's faith, whether that of a saint or that of a lowly sinner seeking redemption, little more than a will to believe that the thought of God will one day become manifest in His presence?

For no idea about God has verily anything in common with the presence of God.

And just as I personally witnessed how the presence of death mocked how I perceived it, I found an ineluctable release in realizing I could truly know nothing of Adonai either.

The holy writ, despite its being judged divinely inspired, I came to understand as the work of devout men using language to sanctify our nature as having been created in the image of the God of Abraham.

In the beginning was the Word and the Word was God.

The Lord of Hosts, I decided, lay beyond all understanding.

A veritable absolute, unsullied by the longings of mankind.

No one could judge me now. Myself included.

* * *

When I passed houses of worship, I no longer viewed them as holy places but monuments to man's conceit at believing himself to have been created in His image. I saw nothing inherently unreasonable about this. Except a caveat should have been appended to those edifices.

That caution might read: HOUSE OF THE MAN-MADE LORD.

How liberating it would have been if I'd viewed Jehovah not unlike one of the ancient Greek or Roman deities I'd read about. How much more magnificent if I could have seen the holy writ in that light . . . instead of trembling at the prospect of incurring His wrath while always coveting His love.

Fear and trepidation coupled with the prospect of a benevolent reprieve merely served to attenuate one's spirit . . . one's imagination.

CHAPTER SIX

SAINT JOSEPH'S SEMINARY

A man who considers life absurd does not dream of being surprised at his individual misfortunes; he regards them as being a confirmation of his theoretical views.[4]

There were no doors marked "EXIT" in the seminary. A closed universe inside God's house. Self-doubt was viewed as a liability—to wit, yours. *Is it pride standing in the way? Perchance you don't belong at St. Joseph's.*

Being discharged was commensurate to being cast out of Eden—a black scourge on your nimbus the remainder of your days.

The priestly theologians brooked no ambiguity.

Yet therein lay my attraction. I willed myself to be unencumbered by other men's beliefs, aspirations, fears, or dictates.

The true condition of man is that of an acrobat who performs above an illusory net, whereas the true believer permits no doubt that the net is God.

Then why perform?

NOVEL EXCERPT

Men with no self-doubt have a "spiritual" air about them: like cash registers, they always ring when you press them.

One encounters very little inquiry in a divinity school. The professors did not principally concern themselves with epistemology, metaphysics, or ontology. Instead, they taught history and biblical interpretation. Texts had to be deciphered in their original tongues. God had manifested Himself in Jesus Christ; now it was simply a matter of wicking it all up.

* * *

Why in Christ's name had I ever ended up here?

Father Eustace Hope, ThD, a five-foot-tall professor of church history who wore elevator shoes and whose head, neck, and torso were carved from a tree trunk, or so it appeared, commenced his lectures with wooden prayers, a Bunraku puppet-like head dangling forward over the lectern for several seconds before it snapped back and the lecture rolled on.

Seconds after he had begun discussing the Canaanites one October morning, the lecture hall's oak doors opened in their cathedral arches: a middle-aged man and young boy entered. As the pair self-consciously sidled along the back wall of the lecture hall, Hope bellowed:

"Nobody arrives late to my lectures!"

"John Gables, class of '47. My nephew Jonathan . . ."

"Have you failed to recall, *sir*?"

"I apologize." Gables turned the boy back toward the great doors.

"For God's sake, man, enough time has already been lost. Sit down!"

Uncle and nephew slumped into the seats nearest them. Hope waited until he felt them properly humiliated. "Where were we, Jenkins, before the *interlude*?"

"You were discussing the Semitic language, sir," the teaching assistant replied.

Gathering my church history, exegesis, and Christian philosophy texts, including the Old Testament in Hebrew—all thick and hardbound—I brought them crashing down on the schoolboy desk and stood. The clap thundered in the vaulted lecture hall.

Hope quivered with rage. "You're excused, Mr. *Mueller*!"

"Have you seen this man before?" I pointed to the visitor.

The students turned their heads.

"*Tell him who you are, sir,*" I said.

Expectant silence gripped the classroom. Hope's grip on the podium suddenly relaxed. He stepped off the rostrum and moved to the platform's apron, first catching his breath. "Who do *you* think he is, Mr. *Mueller*?"

"It's not who he is, sir, but who he *may* be—"

Hope turned to the visitor. "I believe young *Mueller* intimates, Mr. Gables, that you could have been the Christ and I wouldn't have been the wiser. Perhaps if you weren't so clean-shaven . . ."

Several classmates stifled laughter.

"Why are you so sentient, Mr. *Mueller*?"

"I take no stranger for granted, sir."

"What reason would the Son of God have to monitor my class on the Canaanites this morning?"

Jenkins applauded.

"You ridicule my naïveté, Professor?"

"No—it's your righteous arrogance we find amusing. And why came you to St. Joseph's?"

"I saw Christ in a gas station."

Laughter erupted.

"Lost, I presume?"

"I was—in a manner of speaking."

"And you asked for directions?" Hope smugly surveyed the classroom. "Colloquia aside, Mr. *Mueller*, may I suggest that we are theologians here, not aisle dancers. Theology is a science, not a felt show. The Trinity reveals itself in history, not fiction. We ask you and your fellow catechumen to penetrate the sacred texts as scholars, not as weeping fools at a Benedictine shrine. *A Texaco Christ?* Can you sing that doxology for us?"

"Not as mellifluously as you, sir."

I swept the texts off the desk and tramped to the doors. I visualized Hope racing toward me, his miniature legs pistoning him to leap upon my back like a toad to inject his godly poison into my white and impudent neck.

The sound of the arched doors slamming against the adjoining walls ricocheted down three flights of stairs like a cherry bomb in a toilet. I'd addressed one tyrannical self. I was not about to be shaken down by some self-appointed minion of God.

* * *

One evening after the incident with Dr. Hope, I wandered about the quadrangle. I'd blundered in coming here.

And that evening I pulled open the great doors of the lecture hall so that I might enter its massive hallway and cry up its several floors, so empty and dark.

"You up there, Father Eustace Hope. Meet me at the head of these stairs, prick. Stand on your manuscripts if you want so that our eyes may meet, then tell me your secrets. In this sacred darkness, I will tell you mine.

"I want to test you. You and I will climb up the black metal ladder that hangs just outside your lecture hall, the one leading to the turrets. First you and then I will climb up to the slate now glinting in this October moonlight. And it is there—Hope, Faith, Charity—that we will walk to the pediment of this massive brownstone structure and pray.

"You in your sonorous, cathedral-ringing, mellifluous tones and rolled *r*'s about any subject you wish. But soon you must get to the simple question.

"We, old sir, we'll request from your God, the one that brought each of us here, *one* set of wings. Not two, but *one*. A kind of humility and frugality of spirit, don't you think? *He* would approve of that. Yes?

"After you have uttered your prayer, I will one-up you. *I will forgo mine.* For the God I long for is the one who hears people who don't have to speak to him with tongues—no matter how trained in musicality. I won't say a fucking word, sir.

"I will assume He understands my simple need, for it is far down, don't you agree?

"Too bad. No audience. Some are asleep. Others studying church history? And perhaps a few are indulging in matters of the flesh.

"Even here.

"Shame.

"And, sir, we will both leap. I care not whether I go first or second. The test. Which of us will be designated the pair of wings as we dive headfirst into the Boston-paver walkway that girds the great quadrangle?

"Or might we both?

"A *Deather* and a *Lifer*. Ecclesiastical wrens who erroneously presumed they could fly in holy places, this one seventy miles north of Pittsburgh and a couple hundred yards south of hell."

Do I hear you coming up the stairs?

I totter on the pediment, waiting and debating the arc of this act. If I should strip naked and slip at its edge . . . ignominy I own for a brief moment. What does it matter at the lip of darkness how a man swallows his light? Yet, if those are your steps I hear below, for you, I would dive the willowy arc.

With no God strings to feather the fall.

But the loveliest of all gestures to transcend it.

* * *

The lecture hall's granite steps sat mute that night. Unanswered by Eustace Hope. Fitting, for his morning invocations were also met with ghostly silence. The seminary's quadrangle, leached cold under the lampposts. In the morning, its arteries would swell with acolytes trafficking in faith.

Mine had evanesced.

How does one drop out of God school?

Every couple of years, somebody killed himself at St. Joseph's. You could bet on it. A biennial reenactment of the passion of Christ. Either in the dormitory or by a leap off the roof of the lecture hall.

I saw in the eyes of my classmates that something alarming was about to occur. High expectation and demonic glee. As if these lesser human traits had escaped the scrutiny of the righteous ones.

The thalamus of theology.

Feed me before the snow flies and we see a light in the east.

The professors of homiletics and Greek exegesis studied my face too intently of late. "*Mueller*, why so pale?"

Had I not caught them looking straight at me in chapel yesterday? And the president of this august institution—why had he gone out of his way to shake my hand for no particular reason on Wednesday past? "What do you hear from home, Westley?" And wasn't it evident that several in my dorm had been posted at stations on the quadrangle? If I began to climb the hall's granite steps, that tower of Babel, would they not signal the remainder of the community that the black mass was about to commence?

Oh, I could sense it all right. My anguish hadn't abated, and now I carried *theirs*! I had to struggle out of my bed in the morning to attend classes. When called on to recite, I was so filled with foreboding that my tongue thrashed in a pool of mud. "Sawdust in your mandible, Mr. *Mueller*?" Hope took advantage. Others looked upon me with pained expressions. Relief.

Christ was the reward?

If I'd believed, as they did, that some divine being, periodically vengeful, looked after us, perhaps then I could have gone ahead with the wondrous dive to oblivion. *For I would have been only flesh.* The splash of my blood would evanesce to light and spirit, and I would be free of this earthly cage. Happily I'd have accommodated them, even doing a triple flip on my way down into their dervish midst.

But I didn't believe any of it—not one lousy word.

A splat is a splat.

*There are better acrobats
among you. Sorry for the
inconvenience.*
    Westley Mueller

I taped it to my bureau mirror. Then, in disguise as a drunken under-graduate, I lurched out of the dormitory and headed up Merchant's Street, and not until I reached the Coughlin Library did I look to see if I was being followed. But the seminarians were resting in their crisp-sheeted beds—black cloaks hanging freshly laundered on hooks in anticipation of the great day that lay before them.

I would not be the Flying *Mueller*. The community would not cel-ebrate the birth in snow, the garlanded trees, the winking lights—its holy Christmas in peace.

And at six minutes after midnight, I approached the Pennsylvania Turnpike in my Ford.

I had to find Jeremiah.

PART THREE

CHAPTER SEVEN

HUMAN CURIOSITIES

Walking out beyond the seminary grounds that day, I experienced the sensation that passersby were viewing me unclothed. It's something one isn't supposed to do . . . walking away from one's self.

My pace accelerated the farther away from St. Joseph's I got, fearful that someone might yell, "*He's escaping. Catch him!*"

I remember boarding a bus and then exiting at the end of the line in an unfamiliar neighborhood. *No one will recognize me here*, I thought, and then began laughing at myself:

How in Christ's name could they, since I'm no longer who I was? The poor guy vanished like a prayer.

I found a diner and sat in a booth at its far end. The waitress was the first person to speak to the *new* me.

"What can I get you?" she asked.

"Coffee, please. Black, no sugar."

So this is how constructing an identity begins, I thought. Seems normal enough. But what continued to unnerve me was that I'd begun to suffer pangs of guilt for having abandoned myself.

He'd dedicated himself to learning Hebrew and Greek so that he could read the Bible and the New Testament in their original tongue. He'd studied Latin to become proficient in the Roman Catholic liturgy. In the eyes of God, he'd fully committed himself to be among the very best of St. Joseph's priests . . . Father Westley Mueller. Periodically, I'd look out the diner window to see if he might be standing there, peering in at me.

"Hey! You don't get off that easy. It's me, Westley Mueller. Remember?"

I paid the bill and walked for some distance until I entered an area occupied by boarded-up foundries and derelict buildings.

"I don't want Westley to find me," I fretted.

I was startled to see my image mirrored in a windowpane. "Christ, it's him!" I cried, and began running. Soon I was on the outskirts of town with open fields on either side of me. There was no walkway, only an open two-lane macadam roadway.

At some point, feeling both famished and exhausted, I lay down in a field. The sky was overcast and threatening rain.

I could have been praying now, I thought. *Dinner would be served soon. Then to my room, where I could close the door to be alone with my thoughts. The crucifix on the wall above my simple cot. Two wool blankets folded neatly at its foot.*

And as a light rain began to fall and the sky darkened, I tried to fight off sleep, afraid that I'd awaken to my old self lying beside me. I stood and proceeded down the road.

With the rain falling harder, I sought shelter. I passed several large and ancient oak trees but was fearful of being struck by lightning.

On the verge of ignoring that concern, I spotted a male figure walking toward me, pulling a child's wagon. His gait and manner of dress did appear familiar. Once we were several feet apart, the stranger was smiling at me as if we had met in the past.

Where have I seen him? . . . until I realized it was the old monk I'd encountered at Berryville, the one whose stall was graced with plaster of Paris saints, which now sat upright in the red wagon.

Within that senile character and his gilded dolls lay the ineluctable mystery of God, it seemed.

* * *

Brother Stanislaus greeted me like an old friend. I wryly gestured to his Kewpie-doll passengers.

He enunciated each in broken English: St. Benedict, St. Bernard, St. Bruno, St. Stephen, St. Dominic, St. Therese or Little Flower, St. Agnes, St. John of the Cross, St. Lucy, St. Joseph, St. Mary Magdalene, St. Peter, St. Paul, and St. Thomas.

Several were strangers to me.

"Where are you going?" he asked, appearing distressed that the saints had been caught in the rain.

"I don't know," I answered.

"Well, then you must come with us." He laughed.

Brother Stanislaus moved at a rapid pace. The saints jostled together before me like milk bottles.

"Where are we going?" I asked.

"We must hurry," he said. "Any moment now they will appear."

"Who?"

"Our brothers." He said it as if there was no question that I was one of them. Dusk had begun to settle, yet Brother Stanislaus appeared untroubled and kept humming a couple of bars of what I assumed was some folk song from his native country.

As I was becoming afraid that night would overtake us, I saw pale headlights in a distance approaching. They lit up the faces of the saints, ironically exaggerating their lighthearted demeanor. Out of the 1952 Chevrolet sedan stepped the guest master, Brother Paul, in his white hooded cowl, grinning widely and not the least bit surprised at my presence.

"We've been expecting you, Westley. Haven't we, Brother?"

"We just didn't know when," Brother Stanislaus responded, as he began placing St. Benedict et al. on the mohair backseat, but not before drying each one off with the underside of his cowl.

Brother Paul placed the wagon in the trunk of the car, and the old monk and I settled into the front beside him.

Neither of the monks inquired where I'd been or what I'd done since I last saw them. It was as if only yesterday I'd visited the monastery in Berryville. In fact, it was as if time had no meaning for them. Now it was ink-black outside, and the headlights of the Chevrolet cast anemic yellow arcs of illumination before us. Soon we turned down a dirt road, and the passengers in the backseat chattered against each other. At one point Brother Stanislaus turned around and chided, "Please!"

The two monks thought that sublimely humorous, since their order was committed to silence.

The anguish that had preoccupied me earlier concerning having abandoned myself at St. Joseph's and my fear of being overcome by a sense of void had begun to dissipate. "*I may not know who I am or who I am supposed to be,*" I thought. "*But these brothers don't seem to care.*"

For the first time that very long day, I felt strangely at peace. As if I, Westley Mueller, was nothing more or less than those fourteen letters. That neither of the brothers on either side of me was going to require that I become somebody. That I assume a new identity. That I invest years in forging a new persona . . . one that coalesced nicely with theirs.

I was tired of playing a role, especially the one from which I'd just escaped.

The car's headlamps illuminated the familiar wooden gate. Brother Stanislaus got out and swung it open for us to drive through. As Brother Paul waited for him to climb back in, the old monk waved us on, yelling something in his native tongue.

Brother Paul laughed out loud. "The monks tease him about his retinue of saints," he explained. "This way he'll retrieve them once we're inside."

* * *

But I was not prepared for what I saw.

Brother Paul and I entered the refurbished barn where I'd last visited the monastery library. Once inside, he turned and said the following:

"No one enters here who hasn't dispensed of himself as you have done. What you see inside may strike fear in you initially, but it will pass. It's simply that we must embrace the truth of who we believe we are, Westley. Brother Stanislaus carts around those saints not only because he prays to them to intercede in his behalf—that's part of it, of course. What would you expect of a humble, less sophisticated brother like him? But there is something more truthful about each of those figures. If his wagon were larger, there would be even more. He is carting his multitudes of selves about.

"You have crossed the threshold of bidding your first self good-bye.

"Who was that Westley Mueller you walked away from, fearing that he would follow you? You could hear its steps catching up, couldn't you? Yes, it's the same for each of us here. Brother Stanislaus has made it easy for himself. He carts them about. St. Benedict, St. Bernard, St. Bruno, St. Stephen, St. Dominic, St. Therese, St. Agnes, St. John of the Cross, St. Lucy, St. Joseph, St. Mary Magdalene, St. Peter, St. Paul, and St. Thomas. He's attired himself in each of their garments. Mostly in his imagination, of course, while we acknowledge him as simple Brother Stanislaus.

"And in this long hall, which we are to enter, we will lift the scrim of illusion and confront others like you and me and their others.

"Come." He gestured.

* * *

When Brother Paul opened the door, I expected to see monks stationed about the library stacks, as if I were about to undergo some initiation ceremony that I hoped would end harmoniously, given the Christly nature of Brother Paul.

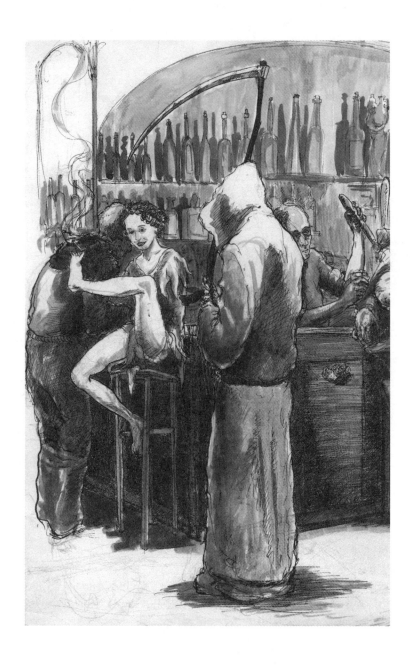

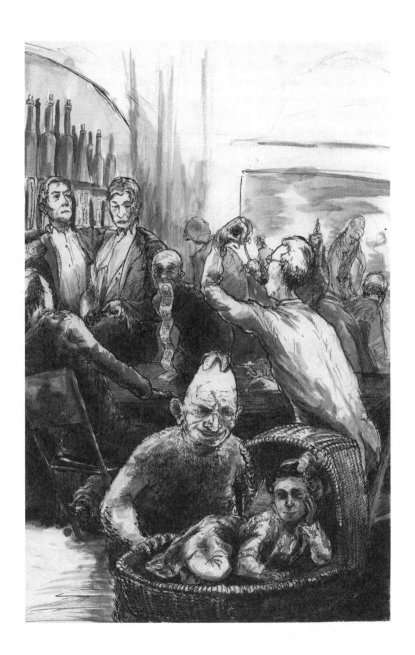

But there was no library. Nor were there monks in the gray working cowls or the brown choir cowls.

Instead I had entered what approximated for me the fabled West End Bar on Broadway, patronized for decades by students and faculty at Columbia University. I, too, had visited there often when I'd briefly lived on 114th Street in Riverside Suites. Late one Saturday, I'd even witnessed Ginsberg, Burroughs, and Neal Cassidy pettifogging there. A Babel of literates is how I saw the eating and drinking establishment and felt as if I belonged, even though nobody knew me or could have cared less. Being there, I absorbed its character all the same.

* * *

In the corner of the large room, two brothers of Asian descent sat alone. Curiously, despite all the extra room about them, their bentwood chairs were nestled next to each other.

They smiled a greeting that indicated we had met before.

I turned to look at Brother Paul for some guidance, but he had disappeared. One of the brothers asked if I had "any smokes."

I shook my head. The other shrugged and gestured that I sit down.

"The Bunkers," they exclaimed in unison. "Chang and Eng."

At which point Chang gestured to Eng to get up and fetch us each a drink.

Eng declined and said, "No, it's your turn."

Then they both doubled over in laughter and stood up, connected by a nine-inch ligament, which could stretch somewhat beyond that, at their chests.

"What'll you have?" asked Eng.

"A whiskey," I said.

"Three Jack Daniels!" he shouted to one of the many bartenders.

Like the two monks, neither of the brothers wondered why I was sitting opposite them. In fact, it felt as if we knew more about each other than was apparent as we sat there conversing. Eng, who was quite pleasant and had a good sense of humor compared to his more choleric brother, mentioned he'd been sick earlier in the day, to which Chang countered that he'd felt just fine. Apparently their wives, Sarah and Adelaide, were awaiting them at home, but neither man appeared too concerned.

"The shows wear us down," Chang groused. "Here we can be ourselves."

At that, he gestured to a person sitting alone at a table alongside us. "Alberta," Eng whispered. "Albert," Chang corrected.

My view was partially obscured by the Bunkers bending toward me, but I could see under the neighbor's table and spotted one foot wearing a man's shoe of average length and the other modeling a diminutive woman's high heel. When I looked up, I saw a face whose left side was lacking any semblance of whiskers and appeared soft as a woman's, while the right side was hirsute and coarse. What I could view of the body above the table line indicated that the person was half man and half woman. Buxom on one side, flat as a skillet bottom on the other.

Eng, bending himself and his brother close to me once again, pointed to their chests while gesturing with his eyes to our neighbor's and molding his hand as if about to cup a breast . . . *sotto voce* pronounced: "Birdseed."

"Birdseed?" I asked, flummoxed.

"A gaffe," Chang replied. "His breast is birdseed."

"Not Adelaide's," Eng japed.

* * *

I politely excused myself and headed to the bar.

"*Whadizit?*," a voice behind me called out. I turned, spotting a man with huge ears and a bald head resembling a dunce cap, atop the point of which rose a tuft of black hair cinched by a purple ribbon. He was covered in fur, but even in the dim light of the establishment it looked like a union suit. He held out his hand to me.

"*Whadizit?*," he said, grinning wide.

I had no idea how to respond.

Appearing at his side was a nattily dressed man I guessed was no taller than two schoolhouse rulers. He pulled at my trouser leg. "It's his name," he advised in a high-pitched German accent. "We call him Zip. Mine is Hans . . . and yours?"

"Westley," I said. "Westley Mueller."

Whadizit? began laughing.

"Why is he laughing?" I asked Hans.

"He thinks your act is funny. Watch his." At that, Hans jumped up on a chair, put his fingers to his lips, and gave a shrill whistle. The patrons around us fell silent.

"Zip is going up for more rounds. Anyone thirsty?"

A man in a tuxedo and nine feet tall tossed Whadizit? a coin. "Schlitz!" he cried.

Whereupon the pinhead tossed it back.

A bearded lady who had sat down alongside Albert/Alberta winged a coin at Whadizit? and cried, "Schlitz!"

The convivial patrons began following suit. Soon Whadizit? was fielding coins for Schlitz from all corners of the ersatz West End Bar and tossing them back just as rapidly.

I looked to Hans for an explanation. But he was now sitting in the lap of a lovely woman of normal height, engaged in an amorous embrace.

Whadizit? stared at them wistfully.

He saw the look of befuddlement on my face and pointed to me, exclaiming "Schlitz!" as others joined him in laughter.

It was only then that I noticed in addition to the ribboned tuft of hair on his dome, he wore half of an orange peel.

Whadizit? affectionately placed his arm about me and introduced me to other "human curiosities" or "living wonders" around the room. I met the Great Waldo, outfitted in formal wear, who would swallow white rats and bring them back up alive and kicking; the Living Venus de Milo, who was born armless but was at the bar holding a lit cigarette between her toes on one foot and drinking from a bottle of beer with the other; there was Prince Randian, the human torso, who lacked arms and legs but was married and had five children.

"My new friend Schlitz," Whadizit? would greet each patron before identifying them. He even led me over to a baby carriage parked at the end of the bar. "Serpentina, pleased to introduce you to my dear new friend, Schlitz." Inside lay a diminutive woman devoid of any bones in her body except for her cranium and a couple in her arms. "Welcome," she smiled. "You new around here, Schlitz?"

She and Whadizit? thought her remark was hilarious, and the wicker carriage literally shook with mirth.

When I asked her if I could buy her a drink, she graciously asked for absinthe.

* * *

I had begun to feel very much at home with these new friends. I liked my new name and how they immediately accepted me as one of them. Perhaps because I was so unlike them physically, I was a "human curiosity" too.

I left Whadizit? assisting Serpentina with her green liquor and wandered back to Eng and Chang's table. Chang, dyspeptic as before, was complaining about the din in the room, inquiring why everybody always had to be chattering, while Eng grinned and said he liked how Whadizit? had christened me.

And as I sat across from the two brothers, I couldn't help thinking that I had a brother too, one I was equally attached to . . . yet mine nobody could see. But Jeremiah was as present at that table, I believed, as I was, sitting across from Chang and Eng. I never went anywhere without him. Yet we were just as dissimilar as the conjoined Bunker twins. At various moments while watching them, I found myself thinking I was in the proverbial hall of mirrors, seeing Jeremiah and me. The true reflection of what only I knew beyond any doubt. There were two of us. Nursing a drink, I'd occasionally glance over at Albert/Alberta and we'd exchange knowing grins of recognition. He was not in the least strange to me, but instead a visual manifestation of how I'd often felt while wearing the chasuble emblazoned with a cross of gold on its back and sweeping up the aisle of an empty sanctuary at night, the incense still wafting in the air from a late holy mass. There were moments I'd felt very much like a seraphic woman under that garment.

I had begun to experience a sensation of liberation.

Whadizit? came over to our table and pointed to the door that led off the bar. Standing there was Brother Stanislaus, who was trying to attract my attention. He gestured me over.

Passing in front of the bar again, I heard the bartenders shout "Happy hour!" At that moment, every bar denizen became mute, focusing intently on his or her image in the gigantic mirror that ran the counter's length. I, too, became mesmerized by what I saw. Each of the "living wonders'" images projected normalcy. They looked no different from those strolling the midways outside the circus tents, the special attraction booths, the so-called freak shows.

Suddenly the tables behind them became silent as if happy hour was a moment of reflection, a kind of memorialization. The bartenders stood immobile. I didn't know what to expect and dared not look anybody in the eye. Even Whadizit? seemed fascinated by his image of normality, as if it were his long-lost brother staring back at him. The one who had died, or maybe whom he had simply been told about, or yet again perhaps it was his imaginary brother, the one he missed more than any living thing.

It was the Living Venus who broke the spell, bursting out laughing, whereupon all the others joined in. Caught up in the expression of exuberance, patrons began tossing coins at Whadizit? once again, while he flung each one back just as the reflections in the blue-tinted grand bar mirror turned normal once again.

Brother Stanislaus now stood opposite me. "Come," he said. "I've got something to show you."

He opened a door that had the markings of an entrance portal to a sanctuary; as I was about to enter, Whadizit? hollered, "Schlitz!" I turned.

"We go on soon. Hurry back."

CHAPTER EIGHT

"FRERE, IL FAUT MOURIR."[5]

We go on soon?

Perhaps Whadizit? and I were a duo routine. He would call my name and begin laughing, and the customers would join in while tossing him coins that he would hurl back, crying "Schlitz!"

A performance not unlike the one I'd been living.

Give me a role that simple men like myself can understand. Build a little box on which I can stand and permit passersby to ridicule me. If it be flagellating to express my eternal damnation, that is just the performance I can comprehend. So when they point and laugh, I can do the same.

Why include me in a narrative that I can't live up to, and when I've tried I failed? The concept of God's love simply overwhelms me . . . where a woman's or a brother's does not.

Whadizit? said we were to go on soon. In this world and not a mythical other place no living being has ever experienced.

* * *

"You are lost in thought," Brother Stanislaus said as he led me down a dark passageway, which opened into a large courtyard that I assumed was the monastery's cloister. He pointed to one corner, yet I could see nothing but several mounds of dirt. As we moved closer it became apparent that these were freshly dug graves, and once we were alongside them, we witnessed monks sitting in them, lashing themselves with disciplines and crying, *"Frere, il faut mourir!"*

"It's when they are the most happiest," Brother Stanislaus explained.

The hooded monks flagellated themselves with acute intensity, as if they were beating molten ingots into some preconceived shape. In this case, Christ . . . or his facsimile.

I recalled Thomas Merton describing his earlier dissolute life in *The Seven Storey Mountain*:

I was stamping the last remains of spiritual vitality out of my own soul, and trying with all my might to crush and obliterate the image of the divine liberty that had been implanted in me by God? With every nerve and fibre of my being I was laboring to enslave myself in the bonds of my own intolerable disgust. . . . But what people do not realize is that this is the crucifixion of Christ: in which He dies again and again in the individuals who were made to share the joy and the freedom of His grace, and who deny Him.[6]

I thought, *Men longing to transform themselves on the smithy of their souls.*

"When will they stop?" I asked.

"At dusk, they return the soil to the graves and carefully put the sod back in place, and then it will resume once again tomorrow with new penitents. But I brought you here to see what is soon about to occur. Wait here."

Brother Stanislaus disappeared into one of the many entryways encircling the green.

He reappeared, pulling his wagon of the enshrined. Accompanying him, a white-cowled monk transported a man-sized scale with a round glass face. They made several more trips, then set about erecting a tiered stand on which they stacked the ceramic saints. Alongside it they situated the scale.

"It's not all tedium inside here." He smiled broadly.

And as I watched the monks climb out of their graves and begin to shovel them full again, others commenced entering the green, shouldering timber crosses that overshadowed their stooped bodies. Each positioned himself at a designated spot in the courtyard and, after stripping to a loincloth, lowered the base of the cross into the ground. (Reservoirs lay disguised under the sod for this ritual.) Within moments, a dozen monks had strapped themselves to their roods.

This is the crucifixion of Christ: in which He dies again and again in the individuals who were made to share the joy and the freedom of His grace, and who deny Him.[7]

The comment made by Brother Stanislaus—"It's not all tedium here"—unsettled me as I watched these men assume the positions of the narrative at Golgotha. Periodically, the voice of one would ring out across the courtyard:

"Why have I forsaken Him?"

This refrain continued throughout the evening. The only illumination as night fell upon the hanging men in loincloths was that coming from the votive candles in various colored jars illuminating the weight guesser's stall. He stood impassively beside the scale as if he were on a midway awaiting the crowds that never showed.

I sat in one corner of the green, transfixed by this pageantry and the fitful sonorous lament. My perception was that these were coveted roles assigned by the abbot to those he deemed the most devout members of the religious community. Yet they marked the passing hours as if they had murdered Christ within themselves again and again.

At intervals throughout the night the abbot reappeared, brandishing a long rod on whose tip hung a metal cup. Upon filling it with water, he would lift the cup to the lips of each monk. The official sentry, Brother Stanislaus, stood alone in his stall with the flickering faces of the ceramic saints stacked behind him.

* * *

I thought about the room I had recently exited, with the living curiosities mingling and relishing their time with each other, knowing that soon they would have to return to acting out their roles on midways set up in meadows and cow fields just outside town limits. There would be a barker outside their tents cajoling fairgoers inside.

Juxtaposed with that memory was what I now witnessed: monks reliving the death of God's only begotten Son while experiencing celestial joy at having been selected for this role they would perform from dusk until sunup.

I read their lamentations as the yearning of the consecrated to hoist themselves out of their bones, their flesh, which burdened their souls and hindered them from ascending to another place. I envisioned them dragging their bodies about like veritable crosses.

As if their enacting of the crucified Christ was liberating, and as if, come morning, each, in a state of euphoria, would feel cleansed, after twenty-four hours without sleep.

At some point I'd become aware that I wasn't the only outside witness to this spectacle. Far to the left of me, in one of the entry-ways, huddled Albert/Alberta. Shortly I saw the Living Venus de Milo slip in, and in her shadow Whadizit?. One living curiosity and then another. Randomly, as if they hadn't conversed with each other, sitting separately, mesmerized by the cries punctuating the darkness while Brother Stanislaus looked on.

As if the cries were uttered on their behalf . . . perhaps even mine. That the keening might carry us aloft.

Surely another hour must have passed when the lamentations began to give evidence of a draining stamina. They had in fact become more melodious and had begun to meld into one collective supplication for release. I couldn't help imagining that the petitioning monks were now sensing that only their voices remained, that they, in fact, were singing themselves out of their pilloried bodies. There existed a tangible air of gratitude, of thanksgiving, in those more harmonious sounds. As if they felt, in some heightened hallucinatory awareness, that they were escaping, cry by cry, out beyond their parched throats and lips. And come daylight, their bodies would be left to unshackle themselves and tramp back into their monastic cells.

It was then that I heard a rustle and turned to my right to see Cleo, the normal and lovely wife of debonair two-school-rulers-tall Hans, pushing the baby carriage before her. Unlike the others, who sat partially disguised in various entryways about the courtyard, Cleo rolled the buggy directly among the crosses before sitting down and lifting Serpentina upright to witness the incantation.

I couldn't speak for the living curiosities, or even Cleo, as to why they maintained a prayerful attitude—as did I—in the presence of the multiple witnesses to the crucifixion.

Except to say that, independent of the monks' liturgies and the practices of the church to which they belonged, the images of twelve men who had bound themselves to timbered roods upon which they sang "Why have I forsaken Him?" throughout the night spoke inscrutably to a longing that each of us is unable to quell.

And in the adjoining room, the Great Waldo was downing the final libation before he returned to his designated role of swallowing white rats. Or the Eng brothers echoing "You first" as they accompanied each other to the tents.

What was my place in this constellation?

But I must have dozed off, for when daylight broke, the green was refulgent in the morning sunlight, with no sign of the living curiosity audience, a dozen men on crosses, or fresh sod over the monks' graves.

Even Brother Stanislaus's booth had been struck.

He was nowhere in sight.

CHAPTER NINE

WE LIVE TO AUDITION

These coveted Calvary roles were the apogee of any monk's life. How one's soul must have thrummed when the announcement came from the abbot and the grudging congratulations, wordless of course, from the other monks.

And it came to me that just hours earlier I, too, had stepped out of the identity I had borne with me for decades.

Except this day I am no longer *him*.

Last evening, as I watched the living curiosities witnessing the Calvary spectacle, I imagined that Albert/Alberta was somebody other to himself than the person who wore a lady's size four shoe on one foot and a man's size nine on another. Or Serpentina, her head held up by the lovely Cleo, listening to the monks' lamenting; surely she wasn't the *lusus naturae* "mermaid," the role that others had assigned her.

And Whadizit??

Weren't we all, that night, questioning the identities into which we are ostensibly locked? Perhaps that's what the living curiosities in the ersatz West End were letting me in on when Whadizit? christened me Schlitz.

And now I'm beginning to suspect *we live to audition*.

The priest persona had legitimacy for several years. I felt totally at home in that identity, comforted by the authority of the scriptures, the generations of ecclesiastical decrees and teachings, the personal gratification that I was experiencing, having been created in the image of God. And there were those rare occasions when I believed I personally communed with the spirit of Christ within me.

Some might inquire: "How can you be addressed as Father Westley Mueller one day then Schlitz the next?"

Yet Schlitz, in the eyes of some, has as much legitimacy as Father Westley Mueller in the eyes of others. The question we must ask ourselves is this: *What is the final worth of living?* How many of us are living in roles that have outlived themselves, ones that are little more than ethers of someone who was once alive?

* * *

When I watched my living curiosity acquaintances scarcely illuminated by the lights in Brother Stanislaus's stall, I felt that each, albeit for a short duration, had, through the intermediary of the monks' cries, risen out of themselves to become someone other than who they were.

Perhaps I was not going to perform the high-wire act of disseminating to others the love of God who gave his only begotten Son so that we might be saved. The consolation is that now there is neither a high wire nor the net . . . and I rejoice in that liberation.

My breath is my own.

I am no other but myself.

I pray only to myself for forgiveness. And perhaps one day for mercy.

So be it.

CHAPTER TEN

HOLY-SCHLITZ

But Whadizit? was nowhere to be found. Cleo and Serpentina and the baby buggy—they, too, had disappeared. Eng and Chang, the Great Waldo, Venus de Milo, even the monastery courtyard that had been surrounded by various entryways and windowed façades . . . vanished.

I was back on the desolate road where I'd encountered Brother Stanislaus the previous day.

As I continued to wander the gravel roadway, it felt as if I were pulling my new friends in a cart or farm wagon behind me. They had christened me, and as long as I could look about and see them, I knew I'd never be alone.

Perhaps that was why Brother Stanislaus always wore that enigmatic smile.

Then it occurred to me:

I could be who I once was . . . except as Schlitz! Someone who strives to make sense of everything, who has an answer for all of life's ills.

I'd act it with such earnest sincerity that folks would find me amusing.

I would fabricate a resplendent chasuble with a *vade mecum* embroidered in gold, wear red shoes, and affect a supercilious air.

Brother Stanislaus could give me pointers.

And as the afternoon wore on, I concocted little skits I could engage in with those who would gather around me on the midway.

I'd wield a censer, releasing its intoxicating fumes from one hand and ringing bright altar bells with the other, and make light of how devout and God-fearing I was. I'd stand on a box so I could look down on them as I made my pronouncements.

First the onlookers would be uncertain how to respond to my spectacle.

All I had to be was someone I once was.

The Confessional:

The confessional with wheels would roll up and down the midway, taking one- or two-sentence confessions, anonymous of course, for a dime. The booth would be fitted out with sacristy bells on either side and *Holy-Schlitz* in neon bright letters affixed to it. At an appointed time, I'd exit the box to "pontificate" on the terrible things I'd heard inside.

Whadizit? could ring the sacristy bells as if it were an ice cream wagon.

Time and again, my refrain when speaking to the midway gathering would be, *After all, how can you be happy and have any real peace if you are not mortifying yourself?* [8]

At which Whadizit? would stare at me, stupefied.

* * *

The Mirror:

One of my presentations would tell of an aged monk going mad in a monastery.

Sometimes he would fight and shout: "No more rule for me!" Then he would break down and sob and say, "I tried so hard to love God, and it didn't work." Father Gerard would give him a shot. [9]

Perhaps I could enact his anguish, accompanied by Whadizit?.

As night approached, I thought about how I'd have Whadizit? pull alongside me a body-length mirror on wheels concealed by a brightly colored tapestry. We'd wander through the midway, declaring: "The Real You. One Thin Dime."

Whadizit?, cajoling a person to give him the coin, would then position him before the veiled looking glass. I'd ring sacristy bells to gain attention and dramatically pull back the curtain. The gathering of course would break out laughing, as the subject's image would be grotesquely distorted.

After one or two stops, with the audience expectation that the next one would be identical, Whadizit? would gesture for me to hand him a dime, which he would then mime handing to himself before stepping in front of the mirror.

He primps before it, miming powdering his face and combing his nonexistent hair in anticipation of seeing himself.

He of course provokes smiles and some laughter.

At which point I unveil the tapestry and Whadizit? views himself in a normal looking glass . . . and he is aghast. His expression mirrors that of the monk who goes mad in the monastery.

He quickly draws the tapestry back over the mirror. We move on.

* * *

Message from God:

With considerable fanfare, I am shrouded then prostrate myself on the mobile confessional.

A banner is dropped from above my head, reading: *MESSAGE FROM GOD.*

Whadizit?, in proper obeisance, kneels down before me to receive the communication, intently concentrating with his ear to my lips while he, Whadizit?, mouths the words so the onlookers can see. When finished, I require him to repeat it back to me.

Satisfied that he has heard properly, I bless Whadizit? and send him on his way.

He carries the *"MESSAGE FROM GOD"* sign as he attempts to find the right party to give it to. But of course there is none. He becomes markedly dismayed as he navigates the onlookers before him, trying to get through them, stumbling en route.

"It is for you!" he cries.

"Me?" an onlooker responds.

"No, *you!*" Whadizit? answers, continuing his quest.

* * *

I played all these skits in my head, anticipating how Whadizit? and I would be star attractions among the "living curiosities."

I reflected on how it was as if Father Westley Mueller had been Holy-Schlitz's leaden self, one that he had to sadly abandon. *And, dare he say it . . . wondered aloud if his predecessor's persona was in truth carrying about the corpse of God within him.*

Yet who would be the first to utter it?

One could envision carrying a dead Christ around within himself . . . but God?

Those twelve mortifying themselves on the crosses, or burying themselves in freshly dug graves, the incantatory cries of the believers that night, with the living curiosities looking on . . .

Was it not some unspoken recognition that God had died within them? Was not the passion of their collectively sung misery reflective of that truth? The verity that no one dared to voice?

Had the freaks acknowledged that among themselves . . . and is that why they neither grinned nor cried but looked on with an expression of wistfulness as if they recalled a period early on when all men were living curiosities, as was God?

* * *

It was then in the inky black that I realized the only light was that inside my head. Yet there I stood in forlornness, lit up in a poignant memory but unable to see my hands before my face. Yet I was still Schlitz . . . or was I?

To whom could I return as Schlitz . . . Jeremiah would not recognize him.

And in the exuberance of abandoning the Father Westley Mueller persona, I became painfully aware that I'd forgotten my brother. In my joy at being able to look back on St. Joseph's seminary with relief and meeting my new friends, the living curiosities, and then being swept up into the spectacle in the monastery's courtyard . . . I'd forgotten my other half, Jeremiah.

As if I'd no longer had a heartbeat.

And in this state of abject terror, I walked back in the direction from which I thought I'd come. Except I had no true sense of where that might be. I had auditioned for a role that had no past or future, one that only was, and for which there were no anchors, other lives.

I'd opted for skit maker, a harmless thespian.

But who was I now?

What were my memories worth to Holy-Schlitz? He was not attached to any of them in truth. Whereas Westley Mueller had been intimately connected to each memory.

In this extreme state of anxiety, I stopped walking and considered whether in truth I might be dead.

That's when I began hysterically laughing.

Dead? Holy-Schlitz?

Dead like the corpse of God within me?

And cried out, "Why have I forsaken myself?"

"Jeremiah," I yelled. "Where are you?"

* * *

And there before me lay the portion of the monastery courtyard where the monks had buried themselves earlier that day or two days earlier.

The rectangles of sod lay freshly in place over the graves as if they were winter blankets. Having fallen to my knees, I stripped one away. The soil was of course not compact, and handful after handful I scooped to the side of the grave. Calling for Jeremiah to rise up and greet me, for I'd seen them lay him down.

Gradually the mound of soil began to rise and the cavity at my knees grew deeper and wider. I sank into it as if it were a tomb. Soon I would hear a faint echo as if Jeremiah were returning my voice.

"Brother, we must not die."

For flesh turns to granite and the recollection of one's sweet breath on one's face is little more than the draft of a closing door. The corpse of God smothers us in such repasts, Jeremiah. Come alive, my voice; give me back my name.

As if I had to summon the strength to roll the corpse of God to one side so that he might begin to stir. And as the water began to return to his eyes, causing him to weep mud and saliva bubbling at the corners of his hoary lips that had begun to blush blue-red, soon stuttering bits of words that rang blasphemous inside his grave:

"Brother, we must not die."

EPILOGUE

PART ONE

My room is not much larger than the one I occupied in Riverside Suites, except here the window looks out upon a glade of aspen trees. When it is pleasant outside, I walk the grounds and spend time with my thoughts. The staff is considerate and kind.

The irony of being cared for by Franciscan monks is not lost on me. But I don't talk about my past. It lies on my dresser, several hundred pages of it, bound by twine. The faded photograph alongside it is that of my father as a very young man.

It was he who brought me here, for I had despaired of finding Westley.

"You mustn't give up your quest" were his last words to me.

That manuscript is the promise of tomorrow for me. By that, I mean it augurs chapters that as yet haven't been composed. For now it is sufficient that I tried. One might even say I lost myself in pursuing him to prove to each of us that I was very much alive and worthy of his admiration.

When guests are invited onto our premises, there are days I expect him to appear in my doorway. He will confess how physically close we were to each other at times.

And I will ask, "Why didn't you speak my name, Westley?"

The promise of tomorrow, he will answer.

* * *

But I have become accustomed to this place, their way of life. Those days when I wish to be left alone, nobody knocks on my door.

Brother Alexander is my closest confidant. It was he who took me under his wing, so to speak, when I arrived at the sanitorium. My father told him I was a writer, to which he replied that we had something in common because he had once starred in the theater. "Small roles, mind you," he demurred. "But I was a very good character actor."

And the three of us laughed.

"What do you write?" he asked during that first meeting.

Papa looked at me expectantly, not certain what I'd say.

"A mystery," I said. But quickly added, "Not the conventional kind, however."

Brother Alexander nodded, muttering to himself, "Yes, that's why we're here."

It was at that moment that I truly felt welcomed in this place.

Within weeks of my arriving, there were moments when I imagined we had known each other in the past. As Westley had made up characters in his stories, I viewed Brother Alexander as one who created roles, with the only difference being that he performed them. When we spent afternoons together, often he would adopt a different personality and keep in character the entire time. I engaged as the situation required. Sometimes his chosen persona was especially angry over some perceived wrong inflicted upon him. Once he wept uncontrollably for an imagined slight against another brother in our community. "It's why we are here," I consoled. "No one takes offense at anything we might say or do." Yet my words did nothing to allay his grief.

Most personas he assumed, however, were quotidian, man-in-the-street sorts, a bit down-at-the-heels, a touch sad and fatalistic in nature, gently self-mocking.

When he came to my door, it was rare that I didn't welcome him to enter. Also, he had a peculiar knock . . . Morse code for "SOS!"

* * *

One day, Brother Alexander inquired about the manuscript on my dresser. "What is that?" he wondered. "Is it a book you are writing?"

"No," I said. "Well, it was never meant to be."

"My characters are never so opaque," he chided, and was about to pick it up.

"Please, don't."

He looked miffed.

"It has nothing to do with you," I said. "It just isn't what it appears to be."

"Then tell me, Ethan."

I took a deep breath, uncertain whether I was prepared to reveal my story even to him, with whom I'd begun to feel close and trusting. But Brother Alexander wasn't prepared to let me escape his penetrating gaze.

I walked to the window and studied the aspens. Soon their limbs would be bare and snow would straddle the north side of their trunks.

Without facing him, "It's not my manuscript," I said. "It is, yet it isn't. I find it very difficult to put in words just what those pages represent."

"But you said you were a writer," he protested.

"I am, in the sense that I talk to myself in sentences, paragraphs, whole chapters that I compose."

"Are you suggesting that stack of papers is composed of notes to yourself, nothing more?"

"No. There is a story inside those pages."

"Well, then you are a writer. Similar to the characters I make up. Except mine I don't put on paper." Brother Alexander tapped first his heart then his head.

I sat down across from him. "That afternoon a week ago when you sobbed without restraint . . . you knew that person well, didn't you? I mean to say it wasn't simply for my entertainment."

"No. It wasn't."

"Because he was you that day, isn't that so?"

"Yes."

"And the following day, when you were that simpleton who sold newspapers at the train station, how you affected that man's stutter, expressing his longing for the affection of a woman he imagined . . . you weren't just doing that for my amusement either, were you?"

He shook his head.

"Well, now I feel even closer to you than before. Because that manuscript over there is remarkably similar to those very personas you invent, longtime friends whom you carry around and visit with in my presence. I welcome and understand them just as I embrace your friendship."

I lifted the book off my dresser, handing it to him.

"In effect, this is that glade of aspens outside my window," I said. "My anchor. The materialization that I, Ethan Mueller, exist. I can hand it to you and say, 'This is me.' For when you shake my hand or place your arm about me in friendship . . . what are you touching? We never know from one moment to the next, do we, dear friend?"

Brother Alexander tucked the manuscript under his arm and embraced me. No words. And I didn't see him for an entire week, not at my door, at the communal table, or outside in the brisk autumnal weather.

I had almost begun worrying about him.

Then one morning before sunup, he signaled "Help!" on my door. I climbed out of bed and opened it. His first words, accompanied by a wide grin:

"Ethan, I am Westley."

* * *

I merely stared at him.

The intensity of his expression caught me off guard. We faced each other as if frozen in time … until I burst out laughing, grabbed him by the arm, and pulled him into my room.

"Only you," I said, "could have pulled that precious moment off."

Except his mien remained unchanged. He placed the manuscript back on my dresser and walked to the window, now with his back to me.

"I apologize," he said.

"For what?"

"What I've put you through."

He's an actor, after all, I thought. *Why not let him continue and suspend my disbelief? Play along.*

Brother Alexander turned to me, stricken. The morning sunlight caused his eyes to glisten like reflecting pools.

"My God, Ethan, I'm lost. Honest to Christ, all that I have believed about myself has been turned upside down."

He sat down on the side of my bed and stared at the wall, his hands racing over each other by turns as if to console, to make amends.

It was a stunning performance. I had even greater respect for Brother Alexander now. It would have been so easy for me to suspend my disbelief. In fact, I thought, *why don't I?* Just to relish the experience.

"Why did I let it go on so long?" he asked.

An actor's rhetorical question, I presumed.

"I want to know what I missed, Ethan!" He was more insistent now. "Couldn't I have been son enough to deliver those stories to him in person? And look what I have made out of your life. Page after page devoted to coming to terms with one Westley Mueller. How do I come to terms with this miserable self I call me? Speak to me, brother. What in God's name have I done?"

* * *

Brother Alexander's self-flagellating performance had begun to unnerve me. I was now beginning to slip back into the life of my manuscript.

Yet he now sat within inches of me, pleading that I reply to him in some manner.

"I'm sorry," I said.

"You are sorry? What have you done except what I've caused you to do? *Please!*"

"No. It's simply too painful for me. I want you to stop playing this character. Brother Alexander, you underestimate your talent."

"You are not getting it, are you?" He reached out and gripped my hand. "*Ethan, I am Westley.* Didn't you hear me?"

An instinct to lash out at him rose up inside me. He had pushed his character acting too far.

"Your little drama's expired," I said, and ushered him out my door.

For several days I didn't see him. Even at evening meals he failed to show. That was not unusual, however, given the freedom each of us was granted. He could stay in his room for days at a time, and when he reemerged there would be no disparaging asides.

* * *

The night that he did appear for dinner occurred on a Friday, always a special event in our weekly habits since the food was more elaborate and accompanied by a better wine than usual. Also, one of us—there were twelve—was expected to provide some form of entertainment at meal's end. Given that the performance was on a volunteer basis only and never announced in advance, occasionally Friday meals closed with two or more presentations.

Another special aspect of the gathering was its formality. A bit ironic in that nothing in the house was ever required, even our right to leave if we so wished. Yet returning without the full consent of those in charge could be problematic. It was not advised. Why risk it? Furthermore, I and the others *had been* on the outside; we liked it here.

We sat at a long, groaning table set with white linen tablecloths and napkins, fine bone china, sterling silverware, and crystal wine goblets. This particular evening's repast consisted of Cornish hens with fresh asparagus and a quality merlot. Other meals were always adequate but perfunctory; we dressed normally and wore name tags identically inscribed: WHO ARE YOU?

The distinguishing feature of Friday's assembling, though, was how one made his appearance at the table. It was the custom for each resident to identify himself in a manner that characterized the life he had lived outside this place. For some residents, it was the shame they carried inside them that they wore to the table. For instance, Father Jeffreys arrived carrying silver lockets that contained photographs of the children he'd molested in the rectory. He would drop them onto his plate, the sound of which unsettled each of us as we assumed his affliction.

Brother Joseph cross-dressed as Italian Baroque painter Giovanni Battista Salvi da Sassoferrato's *Penitent Magdalene*. He entered the dining room as the artist's seventeenth-century devotional painting. With eyes closed and his head resting against a wooden cross, embraced as if it were his lover, the pious resident's long, feminine tresses brushed against his bare shoulders. Assuming his usual place at the table, he'd remain in a fixed position, a *tableau vivant*. Several of us were mesmerized by his presence, but since eye contact was exceedingly rare, at least during gatherings, observations had to occur on the sly.

This habit of not looking at each other in an open way for the most part caused us to always be looking down, say, at our plates or our hands. Sometimes one would espy a resident looking about, but then his gaze would be directed above some other resident's head or at the ceiling.

Upon entering the house, not yet apprised of the tradition, at my first gathering I tried to exchange knowing glances but was summarily rebuffed. In short order I learned, attributing the custom to a sense of communal guilt.

Father Ogden arrived at each Friday's table nude, with nothing but Christ's stigmata painted on him inelegantly with an amaranthine lipstick, the shade of which approximated the nimbus about a black eye. He accompanied that with a grief-stricken mien, that too unchanging throughout the meal. Even when he quaffed the fine wine.

Brother Alexander wore a Trappist choir cowl with a taxidermied white rabbit hanging from its hind legs down his back, suspended from his neck by a leather cord.

Father Dominion, one of the pair of septuagenarians who always positioned himself at the head of the table (he saw to it that he arrived earlier than the rest of us), wore about his waist a luminous St. Francis crimson silk cincture, which he would remove and place before him as if its multitude of capuchin knots were the heads of Biblical snakes . . . yet another convenient focal point for many of us throughout the meal, being that we often kept our heads down.

Brother Rostislav, the other aged resident, carried with him a square box, no lid, containing intricately carved wooden torsos of various saints painted in festive hues, which he would place about his dinner setting like a blockade.

I arrived with my manuscript bound in purple ribbon and clutched tightly to my breast; once seated, I'd place it in my lap for the remainder of the meal. My fellow diners knew that I always carried it on my person outside my room. When passing me in the hallways or outside, each would nod to the manuscript as if it were me.

Generally, the cast as I have described us was unchanging. On occasion, if something troubling or eventful occurred in a resident's life, he would appear in a different guise.

My first experience of this was when Father Louis's father passed away. Previously, he'd always arrived at Friday's table with a silver censer and chain, and at the outset of the meal would light the incense and rise, swinging it over each of our heads one by one. But one night he entered the dining room wearing nothing but a unprepossessing, food-stained silk tie knotted about his neck and a pair of worn spectator wing tips with no socks, which I assume had been his father's. Tied to his left thigh was a white muslin cilice in the shape of a Sacred Heart, which each of us understood had numerous nails sticking out of its reverse side to mortify his flesh. He had exaggerated his lips with clown paint into a garish grin. We never said grace at Friday's meal. At that repast, he rose and wordlessly mimed what we assumed was a blue joke accompanied by scatological gestures, to which we responded to with dead silence. He laughed until he cried.

* * *

On the night in question, I chose not to even sneak a glance in Brother Alexander's direction. At all other meals in the house, the only sounds present were those made by our utensils coming in contact with our wooden bowls. On Fridays, the silver rang against the bone china, and it tended to add a lighthearted air to the occasion.

Invariably, the surprise of the evening was the performance, which of course was never announced beforehand. No one knew since each was voluntary. Did that mean there were Friday evenings with no presentation? I had never experienced one, I suspect because we were all so conditioned to expect something to occur. I couldn't imagine one of us not stepping up to the occasion.

After the meal was over and the table cleared, we were always served a brandy in a snifter glass, and then the expectancy began to grow. You could feel it rise about you. At any change of position by one of the residents, all heads would turn in his direction as if he were about to be the star for the evening.

But this night nobody stirred. Soon each snifter sat empty, and even the servers stood in the doorway surveying our table questioningly.

Could this be the night when we'd return to our rooms unfulfilled?

It was then I heard a foot move under the table and, looking up, I watched Brother Alexander stand and head toward the upright piano. He had never done this before during my time here. I had no idea what to expect. After taking his place on the piano bench, he placed no music before him and sat there immobile.

After several moments, he began to play. Within seconds I recognized the piece: a flawless performance of the Minuet in G Major from the *Notebook for Anna Magdalena Bach*.

Upon finishing, he left the dining room without acknowledging our respectful applause.

* * *

It took every bit of self-control I could muster to suppress a laugh as I walked back to my room.

My god, I thought, *he's brilliant! It's exactly how I imagine Westley would have played it for Elizabeth Andrews in her music room.*

The remainder of the evening, I sat considering how Brother Alexander had pulled it off. Where had he found the *Notebook for Anna Magdalena Bach*? I had never known him to play for himself or others during my residence.

Despite the grudging admiration I had for him for being such a consummate actor in assuming Westley's persona, I was troubled as to how we could continue to be friends if he insisted on not breaking character. He was now playing with my head. And there was nothing now that I knew about Westley Mueller that he didn't also share.

Prior to falling asleep, I committed to distancing myself from Brother Alexander in the hope that he would once again become himself.

I had no familiar contact with him for several days. At the following Friday's dinner gathering, it was Father Louis, still grief-stricken, who sat down at the keyboard and, dressed as earlier in nothing more than the condiment-stained foulard and spectator wing tips sans stockings, pounded out a raucous version of "Adiós Nonino" by tango composer Astor Piazzolla, written just days after *his* father's death.

Each of us sat, visibly stricken. We exited the dining room as Father Louis remained seated at the upright, now calm.

* * *

That Sunday afternoon, Brother Alexander's code knocking roused me from a reverie on no particular incident but instead a collage of memories in which one seemed to suggest yet another. This had happened with some frequency since I arrived here, and in all honesty, I found the experience to be quite pleasant.

When I opened the door, he appeared especially distressed.

"What is it?" I asked.

"Can I come in?"

He sat on the side of my bed as I sat across from him.

"Ethan, I have something I must ask you. And I expect you to tell me the truth."

"Go on," I said.

"How is she?"

"How is who, Alex?"

"Please. You know very well who I mean."

"I'm sorry. I don't."

"What else did she tell you about me that isn't in your manuscript?"

"You mean the widow Elizabeth from whom you learned to play that sweet little *Anna Magdalena Bach* composition?"

"You are very cruel, Ethan. It doesn't become you."

"Well, she told me what a chameleon you are, Alex. That you insinuate yourself into another's past, learning all you possibly can from them on the pretext that you are their closest confidant . . .

until the day you turn it all against them. Please, Alex, I ask you to leave. I shared my manuscript with you in good faith; now you have callously assumed the identity of my lost brother, turning our wonderful friendship into something very dark and disturbing."

Brother Alexander neither spoke nor prepared to leave the room.

I walked to the door and opened it, gesturing for him to exit.

At that he took from his pocket a folded sheet of paper, handing it to me on his way out.

"Read it. If you wish to talk, you know my room."

Initially, I had no interest in looking at the note, fully convinced by this time that my assumptions regarding what he was up to were correct. What I couldn't square, however, is why was he unwilling to drop his act at the risk of ruining our relationship. Very few of the residents were as fortunate as he and I were. Most felt alienated from each other, and several from themselves.

That night prior to turning in, I decided that reading the note might unravel the mystery. It read as follows:

Dear Ethan,

I have been in contact with our father. He's asked to visit us.

Let me know.

Westley

And on the reverse side of the sheet of paper, he had written:

I was not surprised at your response today, fully expecting to be rebuffed. Yes, there are moments when I question if it wouldn't be better for me to leave well enough alone and remain Brother Alexander. It would be so much easier for each of us that way. But, Ethan, as you recognize by now, life doesn't permit us to narrate our lives as we might wish. You've come to peaceful terms with yours . . . until I decided to remove my mask. I've thought long and hard about it.

Except you appear to have found peace and I haven't . . . and that's because the story must play out in its own time, its own will.

I asked you today regarding Elizabeth. Have you known love? When you were in that room with her that day, Ethan, couldn't you feel my presence? Didn't she telegraph our intimacy to you? Did it not unsettle you? You suggest as much in your manuscript.

Well, that's what I was beseeching you to gift me this afternoon. Yet you spurned me. Are you fearful of having to suffer the memory of such intimacy? And why did she look so fiercely into you that afternoon? Was she attempting to call to life again what you and she had once enjoyed? Is that what you are afraid of, brother?

Think about it.

He had touched on the afternoon with Elizabeth. Her gazing at me as if she were seeking to summon up a memory that I no longer recalled. In all my time seeking Westley, it was those fraught moments in her presence when I anguished that I could have been, and perhaps was, the very person I was seeking.

Was Brother Alexander wise to this?

And why had my father brought me here?

* * *

What I couldn't comprehend was the motivation behind Alex's maneuvers. Any desire to pursue the quest that occupied me for some time had expired. Prior to his reading my manuscript, I had become accustomed to my daily routine, the unchanging nature of my new environment where there were no surprises and each day was indistinguishable from the day before. The other house residents were as self-contained as I in that we enjoyed being alone, outside our coming together for the evening meal. Yet, even then, a vow of silence was in order. I do admit, however, that without those diurnal gatherings, the prospect of being totally alone frightened me. As I suspect it did others.

It had been Brother Alexander who first insinuated himself into my daily routine. Unlike the other residents, he made an effort to get to know me. And in short order I found myself looking forward to his coded knocking on my door.

What most intrigued me about him was his past vocation as an actor. The template for my manuscript was Christopher Daugherty's "Going Dark" story, in which the narrator lost himself in several personas. It was that thread that wound itself through the work's couple hundred pages. And from the start it was sufficiently evident that Brother Alexander was a master at assuming a role so masterfully that he came precariously close to convincing himself, let alone his audience, that in fact he was that individual.

It took me some time to wonder why he was a resident in this house, until I finally concluded that one too many times he'd fallen victim to being kidnapped by characters he performed. Each of us had a reason for our residency here. Except I was not that interested in learning why others were admitted, knowing that at some later point it would be revealed by accident or intentionally. The Friday dinners offered a storehouse of possible reasons for one's admittance.

It was not lost on me that Brother Alexander had fallen into his earlier "sickness" for want of a better word . . . that of assuming a character and then becoming victim to it. I fully believed he had become infatuated with the idea of Westley, the author, and had begun to slowly build that character into which he would eventually slip. Alex had become Westley Mueller throughout every hour of the day now. I had opportunity to observe him with some of the house staff, establishing that he had adopted a character with whom they were unfamiliar.

And the bitter irony is that I had created him.

Now he speaks about our father visiting us.

In truth it would be quite easy for me to concede that he is my brother. What comes to mind initially is that we could now leave this house on our own and go on about our lives. Isn't that what I set out to do? And since he is convinced that he is Westley, and has integrated that character into his very marrow, what is there to lose?

Two brothers reuniting after many long years of separation.

After all, do I have more evidence than not that Brother Alex is indeed my long lost sibling? Furthermore, would anyone actually care one way or another, except possibly our father?

Even then, since it was he who admitted me here, I suspect he'd go along with the arrangement once he saw how compatible we were with each other. *Truth?* What does it matter finally?

But what if, at some point, Alex is able to free himself of Westley's persona? Then I'd have to take that risk. But in the meantime, my manuscript would become alive; we would revisit it and improvise on its pages. We could even seek out Elizabeth if he or I so desired. *Brothers loving one woman?* It's happened in the past. So we share her without trying to hurt the other.

We could write new stories together, he in one room, I in the other, and then share them at dinnertime.

The only difference being that I'm aware Alex is trapped inside his Westley character, while my playing his sibling is a choice and a role that I could at any time abandon.

Why was I resisting what had begun to increasingly occupy my thoughts? I missed the interaction with my friend. So what if he insisted he was who he wasn't? Friday's dinner revealed infinitely more complex and troubled issues. And now that I knew he could play the piano, why, that would bring some needed light into our lives.

* * *

The following Friday, he appeared wearing his choir cowl with the white rabbit hanging down his back. He glanced in my direction, and we surreptitiously made eye contact, a rarity at these gatherings. Nothing noteworthy occurred at this repast; each of us appeared in our customary "costumes."

It was following the cordials while we awaited the surprise performance that tensions spiked. No one volunteered. We must have sat for nearly ten minutes before Father Louis stood up and agitatedly announced, "In all my years here, this has never occurred before. We can't leave this gathering without fulfilling what so little is asked of us. Please."

Yet not one of us could bring himself to perform. It was an unwritten assumption that each performance was to be inspired and not rote. That it was something an individual was truly moved in the moment to do.

I could feel the tension rise in the residents about the table. Each was hoping an inspiration would come as if from God. But we were empty, hollow; only the echoes of ourselves ricocheted within ourselves.

Until Brother Alexander rose and announced:

"We have two distinguished visitors gracing our presence this evening. I couldn't be more pleased to introduce to you, my fellow residents . . ." At which point he disappeared behind a screen for several moments, upping our expectations, only to reappear, bloated like a belly-god, and gesture for me to stand.

"Holy-Schlitz to my left, and yours truly, Whadizit?." At which point he lowered the hood of his cowl to reveal his cone head with the identifying tuft of hair tied with a red ribbon. Whadizit? solemnly bowed, took my arm, and led me over to the piano, where he sat down and played a rousing yet dissonant rendering of "Love for Sale."

Smiles began to break out on the formerly tortured miens of the residents.

One could feel the unease escape from the room. The servers, for the first time in my recollection, refreshed our brandy glasses.

Now Whadizit? and I were to perform. There was no reason for me to anguish over what might occur between us, since I'd witnessed him so cleverly digest every last word of my manuscript. I also assumed that he was fully equipped to improvise on my experience with Brother Stanislaus and the Living Curiosities.

I stood at the table's head and proclaimed:

"After all, how can you be happy and have any real peace if you are not mortifying yourself?"

At which Whadizit? stared at me, stupefied.

It was Father Louis who guffawed, then proceeded to paroxysmally cough in an effort to disguise his mirth. He brought his food-stained silk tie to his lips while standing and exposing the muslin cilice tied to his left thigh. His clown-painted grin of self-reproach accompanied his concealing the flesh-mortifying Sacred Heart with the linen table napkin.

"*I tried so hard to love God, and it didn't work!*" Whadizit? cried.

Now aged Brother Rostislav belly-laughed. The dozen wooden torsos of saints began collapsing, with several sliding onto the floor.

Penitent Mary Magdalene, aka Brother Joseph, scandalized by the incipient levity, shot up without breaking her canvas verisimilitude until she banged the rood on the groaning table in utter disgust, then quickly resumed Giovanni Battista Salvi da Sassoferrato's work.

Chastened, the residents resumed their air of communal guilt once again, even more so.

Whadizit? was not about to be dissuaded. Once more he cried, "I tried so hard to love God!"

Again he disappeared behind the screen, returning with an oversized ear that he attached to one of the screen's muslin panels. And above it a sign reading:

CONFESSIONS IN PROGRESS. SILENCE PLEASE.

Whadizit? assumed the countenance of a priest and pointed to the ear, then to me, as if I were next in line. It was positioned belt-high, forcing me on my knees. He vanished behind the make-believe confessional booth.

I proceeded to mime an agonized prolix confession, and at various points Whadizit? gestured as if he'd never heard anything so vile, so blasphemous, so utterly depraved . . . each expression more aghast, so that by this time the residents had begun audibly laughing. Even Father Louis was inspired to stand and circle the table while swinging his silver censer as if to promote our performance.

By this time I, too, had thrown off all inhibitions and began to gesture obscenities, manifesting a countenance that mocked Magdalene's. Father Dominion untied his luminous St. Francis crimson silk cincture and handed it to me, whereupon I flagellated myself with its multiple capuchin knots while venting into the confessional ear.

But Whadizit? no longer appeared. Soon, in character, I expressed concern and peered behind the screen, only to return looking apoplectic and despairing.

Father Louis, who was also ringing epiphany bells in his trousers, froze, as did each of the diners.

I opened one panel of the ersatz confessional to Whadizit?'s inert body on the floor. Wildly gesturing for assistance, I tried to lift him. Father Dominion and Brother Rostislav, the septuagenarians, came to my aid.

Onto the table, I pantomimed.

Once we laid Whadizit? out, I bent my ear to his chest, hoping for a heartbeat.

But because of his ballooned body, I was having difficulty. I kept trying to press the "stuffing" down so that I might hear better. Only when I reached into his shirt did I begin to withdraw loose ends of what appeared to be adding tape on which were written in heavy red letters the following words: LIES, ADULTERY, GREED, SEX, SIN, repeated continuously.

Now, as if fighting against the clock, I admonished the residents to assist me. Fathers Louis, Ogden, and Jeffreys worked on Whadizit?'s arms and legs, unrolling from his person what seemed to be countless rolls of tape bearing those words.

These covered the table and spilled over onto those still sitting, in a virtual trance, witnessing our efforts to revive Whadizit?.

When his body appeared normal again, I stepped away from the table. The scene had been depleted of any comic cast.

I waited in earnest for my partner's next move.

Slowly, he began to stir one leg, then an arm; he lifted his head and glanced around. Shortly he evinced a crabbed smile and sat up.

"*I tried so hard to love God,*" he uttered.

As if he were testifying for each of us.

Whadizit? climbed down off the groaning table.

He beckoned me closer and whispered in my ear. I resisted, as if offended by what he said. But he insisted.

I stepped away from him and began to look directly at each of the residents. Instinctively, each looked to the ceiling or to the floor, except the "painting."

"He wonders if each of us is carrying about the corpse of God within him," I said.

"Who would be the first to utter it?" Whadzit? challenged.

Their faces mirrored the blank expressions of Father Rostislav's wooden torsos.

He removed the conical pate that he'd carefully fabricated, slid his hood back on, and replaced the taxidermied white rabbit. Brother Alexander summarily abandoned the dining room. Moments later, each of us filed out to the clatter of dishes being cleared and hushed conversation in the kitchen.

* * *

FRIDAY AFTER-DINNER VIGNETTES CANCELLED.

The notice was posted the following morning in the dining room.

House overseers called us in and admonished us for a "blasphemy beyond reproach," was how they phrased it. When asked what our defense was, Brother Alexander said there was no malicious intent on our part, but when the residents began to become so animated and robustly alive in a manner he had never witnessed . . . "well, I just lost it."

"Lost what?"

"Asking the question that must never be uttered."

"And having done that?" they persisted.

"I feel as if I've crawled out of a grave."

The overseers looked at each other, nonplussed, speechless. Brother Alexander stood. "I'm sorry," he said, and together we left the room. Neither of us spoke to each other for several days. It was evident that we had caused considerable torment in the interior lives of the remaining residents. To a person, each appeared to have visibly compounded the guilt already encumbering them. At meals they chose to close ranks, forcing Alex and me to eat at one end of the table by ourselves.

We were pariahs.

Yet the effect of that Friday night's performance on me was also one of modest liberation. I hadn't dared to address the unutterable that my friend had. But it was as if he rose out of my manuscript and did what I could never have done in an environment like ours. True I had harbored such thoughts . . . *but Brother Alexander spoke them.*

And everyone except he and I figuratively gasped.

Upon returning to my room that evening of the performance, I felt closer to him than I ever had. And as I lay in bed, pondering what we had done, it felt as if he were alongside me, laughing at the delinquent liberties we had taken . . . like two siblings.

* * *

At some point that night, I was awakened by his signal on the door. When I opened it, he stood before me in street clothes, the white taxidermied rabbit dangling from his right hand, the choir cowl from his left.

"Can I come in?"

Years earlier, I'd heard that very same question.

"Get dressed, Ethan."

"But it's the middle of the night."

"I know."

"Where are we going?"

"Home."

I began laughing . . . then he joined in.

"Except there isn't any," I countered.

"I know."

"So?"

"Someone there will recognize us."

I began to get dressed.

"Like who you once were, Ethan. Not who we are here." He reached into my closet, tossing out my street clothes like his. "We have to leave before the others rise."

Once we were outside and began walking toward the town, he looked back and stopped.

"They meant well," he said.

Then, with a wide grin, he turned to me. "What took you so long, brother?"

PART TWO

He looked surprised, discomfited, to see us sitting there.

We were seated at the very same picnic table where he'd given me the box of Westley's writings. Having implied the meeting would be between him and me, I was visibly anxious as to what might occur. Would the true nature of Brother Alexander and my relationship be unveiled when he appeared?

Was Westley the impostor I feared he might be?

The two eyed each other intently.

But momentarily, Papa relaxed and sat down across from us, studying my face for a while before uttering:

"Your mother would have given her life for this moment, Ethan."

He clasped my hands. "You found him. You brought Westley home." Visibly moved, he turned to Brother Alexander.

"I treasured your stories, son, but they were no substitute for your longed-for presence. Before your mother passed on, she asked for forgiveness for having alienated you. When she lost you, she also lost Ethan . . . and because of that, departed in a troubled state."

He parsed his words as if by uttering them he was resurrecting their wounded presence. I was struck by how my own self-absorption had denied each of us what I had in fact been seeking. I also knew that any hope of reconciliation between us was fated.

Yet his departure would not mirror hers.

"That Sunday I sat across from you, Ethan, on this very spot, encouraging you to find Westley and seek his return, yet deep inside I worried it would all end badly. That you would carry out your dark attraction to the bridge.

"Except here you both are, and no longer strangers."

I wanted to speak but sensed in the tenor of his words, how he paced them, that they were chosen carefully so as to not reveal what they were disguising.

It was in that moment that a buried fragment of the stories surfaced in my consciousness:

When he pulled me out of the swells in his seersucker suit and stocking feet, he promised me I wouldn't die. And when he laid me on the sand and pumped my bony chest, urging I give the green water back to the Great Lake, he cried, "You won't die. I swear in God's name. Everything's gonna be OK. Now pass it up, boy. Spit it all back up."

After the panic subsided and I'd begun taking deeper, more peaceful breaths—looking back at the high waves, they almost laughing, *Next time, kid. You were nearly ours*—I turned to my father and saw that he, too, had begun to assume a come-unto-me smile, the very reason I'd entered the water unafraid. Two-tone shoes kicked off several feet away, jacket and trousers clinging to him like wet newsprint, his belt buckle glinting the morning sun—I wondered where he'd come from, for I'd gone to the shore alone that morning.

With a pleasant rain imbuing the sand with a muddy brown and the lake's waves breaking louder, to grow fully awake, I'd decided to walk into the surf when its grainy floor suddenly collapsed and an undertow pulled me out toward the horizon.

Nobody was around. I screamed back to our cottage, the one that sat at the edge of the precipitous drop-off.

Where had my father been?

And why was he dressed so handsomely for the occasion?

* * *

Years later, when I became a man, I recalled that incident and confessed it had caused me to bond to him like a child to a mother. With me in his arms, he'd climbed seventy-two wooden steps up the eroded shore to our rented cottage.

"Miraculously you appeared out of nowhere, Dad, in your blue seersucker suit, your hair slicked back, and that iris tie with a splinter of yolk tearing down its front—Christ, I thought you were the cat's ass."

"I was, boy, until you interfered." His dismay masked a pale grin.

"Interfered?"

"On your way to the stony deep."

"What did I disrupt?"

"Somebody one lane over from ours, waiting in her doorway."

"Another woman?"

"The yard outside our cottage where we played badminton . . . remember how it eroded over the winter and spring each year, and we knew one summer we'd return to the lake and even the rental cottage would be gone?" He rubbed his eyes.

Once the azure of a calm Lake Erie, his irises were now occluded like pearl seeping across blue marble.

"Who was she, Dad?"

"I don't recall," he muttered.

* * *

I'm not sure what precipitated my recollection of this excerpt. Perhaps it was the manner in which he looked at me as if willing me to recall a crucial moment between us. Maybe the trigger was his inferring the bridge lights. Or my attraction to water. Or his deeper understanding that fathers exist to save their sons. For he had that day. I was going to die, but for some strange reason following that incident, I felt a kind of invulnerability.

That he, in a seersucker suit and iris tie with a yolk of yellow running down its center, would remove his spectator shoes and save me. From women, the deep, or myself.

But now he no longer sought clandestine rendezvous. He was an old man. The gentler sex only visited his dreams . . . and even then their lights, their odors, their laughter had dimmed . . . and he'd awaken to savor what he'd once tasted, sung to, held onto for yet one more turn down the hollows of this wondrous arcade.

Would he have known Brother Stanislaus? I wondered.

This moment of recognition between us lingered while Brother Alex looked on. Perhaps each understood what was transpiring more than I did. Yet the memory was mine and mine alone. Even if Westley had penned it.

This was Papa's good-bye.

As if he was saying to me, *My watch is over.*

It was at this moment I sensed I was taking on water, that my lungs were filling with the grief of his departure. And inside me, I witnessed myself calling out to him, as if he were up on the hillside looking down on me. Except I saw him begin to fade. The seersucker suit began to turn primrose like the abundant yarrow at the cliff's edge, his face became obscured by a wispy cloud, and his black hair metamorphosed into a raven that echoed back to me.

And once again I looked across to him . . . *My watch is over, son. God willing, we'll meet up again.* But then he flashed his ingratiating smile.

Except more than likely not.

The Dodgems died yesterday.

* * *

The denouement, however imperfect it might be, had now taken place.

Papa caught my look of panic as to what was actually transpiring. He eyed me as if to acknowledge its truth but to keep it between ourselves.

"You are grown men now. Early on—and to hell with the park onlookers—we would have celebrated by removing our clothes and jumped into icy Big Run, swimming out to where the Lightning Roller Coaster dipped heart-shudderingly close to its deepest part before climbing again. The yellow-and-red cars are no longer operating, but we would have circled the floor manically waiting for the first opportunity to crash headlong into each other . . . laughing in a manner I've forgotten how."

I caught Brother Alexander staring up the hill where as a boy I'd run soon as I wolfed down the picnic lunch to the park's midway and its rides. *Was he recalling his summer afternoons there?*

"What are you remembering?" I asked.

"The lemon meringue pie." He laughed.

Yes, I thought, *my manuscript.*

"I'd like to take you back to our old house, boys . . . but it's empty now. The neighbors have either died or moved away. It began to take too much out of me to keep up. One day, I packed a suitcase and locked the doors behind me."

At that, he placed a key ring on the park table.

I was uncertain as to his intentions.

"It's yours," he said. "You and Westley can fix it up over time. Reclaim your old rooms. I kind of let it go. But with a couple weeks of labor, it will feel and look just as it did when you were growing up there."

I looked over to Brother Alexander.

"Where are you living now?" he asked.

"A tidy little room in town. Closer to a few old friends who are still around and not far to walk from where I get my papers each morning and stop in at the tavern to shoot the breeze and enjoy my morning wake-up."

At that, he stood up . . . as did we. Hesitant at first, he came over to our side of the table, embracing me.

"Ethan, your not succumbing to the jelly jars enabled me to hang around . . . for which I'm grateful. I couldn't have survived knowing that you went off into the so-called Big Run without me in pursuit."

As for Brother Alexander, Father grasped his hands, though he stood a bit formally across from him: "May you find peace here. Your brother needs you. What other reason is there to live? Thank you for bringing him home."

When he was almost out of sight, I cried out:

"Please stop by, Papa!"

"Oh, I will," he muttered.

"At the first sign of summer, we'll challenge you to a race here in Big Run!" Brother Alexander chorused.

Papa turned, and I could detect in the distance a wry grin. It was as if he was deciding how to respond.

"I may have already gone in without your knowing it," he replied. "Always wanted to know what's beyond the Lightning's dip where we always turned back."

ENDNOTES

1. Robert Penn Warren, *All the King's Men* (New York: Harcourt, Brace & Company, 1946).

2. Edmund White, *Genet: A Biography* (New York: Knopf Doubleday Publishing Group, 2010).

3. Paul Bowles, *The Sheltering Sky* (London: John Lehmann, Ltd., 1949).

4. Jean-Paul Sartre, *Saint Genet: Actor and Martyr*, trans. Bernard Frechtman (New York: George Braziller, Inc., 1963).

5. "Brother, we must die."

6. Thomas Merton, *The Seven Storey Mountain* (Harcourt, Brace & Co., 1948).

7. Merton, *Seven Storey Mountain*.

8. Thomas Merton, *Entering the Silence: Becoming a Monk & Writer* (HarperSanFrancisco, 1996).

9. Merton, *Entering the Silence*.

BIOGRAPHICAL NOTE

Dennis Must is the author of two novels: *The World's Smallest Bible* (Red Hen Press, March 2014) and *Hush Now, Don't Explain* (Coffeetown Press, October 2014); plus three short story collections: *Going Dark* (Coffeetown Press, 2016), *Oh, Don't Ask Why* (Red Hen Press, 2007), and *Banjo Grease* (Creative Arts Book Company, 2000). He won the 2014 Dactyl Foundation Literary Fiction Award for *Hush Now, Don't Explain*, and *The World's Smallest Bible* was a 2014 USA Best Book Award Finalist in the Literary Fiction category. His plays have been produced Off-Off-Broadway and he has been published in numerous anthologies and literary journals. He resides with his wife in Salem, Massachusetts.